RHINO CHASERS

Rhino chasers are big-wave boards
designed to tackle the immense power of deep ocean
swells. In an environment where massive waves break on
outside reefs, and surfers paddle out on slabs of foam and
fibreglass to meet them, it is easy to lose control. Big-wave
surfing is about mastering danger, about pushing body and
mind beyond their limits, and entering another world
where fear is no longer an option.

RHINO CHASERS

NEIL GRANT

ALLEN&UNWIN

First published in 2002

Allen & Unwin
83 Alexander Street
Crows Nest NSW 2065
Australia
Phone: (61 2) 8425 0100
Fax: (61 2) 9906 2218
Email: info@allenandunwin.com
Web: www.allenandunwin.com

National Library of Australia
Cataloguing-in-Publication entry:
Grant, Neil, 1966- .
Rhino chasers.
ISBN 1 86508 695 9.
1. Young men - Fiction. 2. Surfers - Fiction. 3. Male friendship - Fiction.
I. Title.
A823.4

Cover and text design by Andrew Cunningham - Studio Pazzo
Set in 10 pt Sabon by Studio Pazzo
Printed in Australia by McPherson's Printing Group

10 9 8 7 6 5 4 3 2 1

ACKNOWLEDGEMENTS

Thank you to: Antoni Jach, Delia Falconer and Sandy Webster for guidance and support; three RMIT novel classes, in particular Dave Cameron, Donna Noble and Julie Peters, for honesty and inspiration; Jenny Pausacker, my mentor, for wisdom and tea; the Victorian Writers' Centre and the Australia Council for my mentorship; Simon Ashford for his editorial eye and surfing knowledge; Eva Mills and Erica Wagner at Allen & Unwin for giving me a go.

DEDICATION

This book is for Ingrid and Emma
who were as much a part of the journey
as Goog, Castro and Aldo.

EAST

1

INDO DREAMING

Goog sat on his board, his waist buried in the sea. Water temperature was thirteen degrees, about normal for this time of the year, and his balls were shrunken into him like hard little stones. There was a light offshore wind lifting spray from the top of the five-foot right-handers that wound over the sand-covered reef. This was a backhand break for the goofy-foot. It always made him nervous to surf with the wave spitting and hissing over his shoulder.

Castro was paddling back from his last wave, searching the horizon for the bulge that would show the coming of a new set. Aldo was a few metres away, too far inside, just begging to get drilled by the set waves. He was pulling at his eyebrow ring, his head blue with cold and new buds of stubble.

Aldo was a year older than Goog and Castro and owned an HQ wagon. Before Aldo's car, there had been Mum and the embarrassment of rolling up at Thirteenth Beach in her old Corolla with their boards poking out of the boot; then waiting for three hours (even if the waves were crap) for her to do her shopping and return. Goog suffered Aldo's moods and his violent temper for the mobility that his car offered.

Castro was different. He was the glue that bound them all together. He saw something in Aldo, something that no one else could. Castro was the sort of guy that was always bringing home strays. It wasn't important to Castro how something was; he cared more about what something could become.

Goog had known Castro since the first days of primary school, when everything had been possible. Castro was the joker, the one who kept the classroom alive and made the teachers earn their money. He was a star who had everyone spinning to him in wild orbit.

Goog lay down on his board and spat thin ropes of hair from his mouth. His hair was a bleached reminder of summer. Now the water brought on ice-cream headaches and Goog found it hard to remember the warmth of four months ago. He could still picture the slow drain of traffic through town – the week-end warriors with dinged-up old single-fins strapped to their Magna station wagons; the throaty gust of big bikes on their way to the Great Ocean Road proving grounds; trendies on weekends away in their Golf cabriolets with the tops rolled back. Yeah, he could picture all that, but he couldn't remember the heat, the sun gnawing his forearms, the water warm enough to wear a springsuit through a two-hour session.

'Your wave, pindick!' Aldo shouted as he paddled hard over the first wave in the set.

Goog turned and began to stroke for the shore. The wave lifted him and he pulled deeply twice more, a left and a hard right, before springing into the crouch. He didn't bottom turn, the wave was too fast and steep; he just ripped a tight line over its face, bending his back knee and pushing the board as fast as it would go. The wall ahead of him got steeper and he could see a narrow white fringe appearing.

'Pull in!' Castro yelled from the shoulder as the wave began to heave upwards, dragging more and more water up until it started to barrel over the heavy sand.

'*Pull iiiiinn!*'

Goog would have to backdoor the tube. He could see an oval of headland framed by the growling sea; it was beginning to close. The wave would shut tight like a steel jaw trap as soon as he ducked inside. He would be pushed hard onto the bottom and it would hurt. Sure it was small, but even small days could be risky. Days like this you could push yourself too hard and get hurt.

He pulled wide just before the wave shut down, blowing up sand and chunks of kelp. Carving back towards the wave, he dived forward into the foam and then down until he felt the tug of his board tombstoning in the rush of white water above. His shoulder scraped along the sand and he turned back up to look at the strange light, the borrowed blue of the sky, the rumbling tide of bubbles.

He surfaced in time to see Castro deep inside a barrel, howling like a wild dog, his face masking up with concentration as he tried to exit. Goog copped the wave on the head, second prize, before it dragged him over the falls backwards. As he dropped, he pushed his board away from him, trying to avoid a slice from the fins.

Churning through his second spin cycle, he finally found air, gulping it down as if it were the most precious thing in the world. He pulled at his legrope but there was no resistance. It had snapped a metre down its length.

Aldo raced by, his face set in a nasty sneer, slicing huge

rooster tails into the air and forcing the wave into submission. Goog snatched a quick breath and dived for the bottom. Too late. The wave caught his legs and sent him cartwheeling through the water. He rose and got a snap at the sweet air and then he was under again. His chest hurt. His wetsuit unzipped and filled with sand and icy water. For one mad moment he thought, *I'm going to die here,* but he relaxed and let his body be tossed and buckled by the sea. It picked him up and, in one final act of spite, drove him heavily into the sand of the shore-break. Stumbling to his feet, he managed to escape the water. He dropped onto the beach beside the dried corpses of mutton-birds. A gang of spidery crabs ran up to him, certain of a meal. A few metres away, his board lay at the high-tide mark, snapped cleanly in two like a cuttlefish bone.

He watched for half an hour as Aldo and Castro caught wave after wave, ducking into tubes, pulling off long floaters. Wave after wave after wave. He sat until the sand felt as cold and hard as concrete and the seagulls strode up to eyeball him with their side-on suspicion. Eventually the wind came up and blasted everything, chewed the ocean into whitecaps and blew sand along the beach like smoke. Goog grabbed his snapped board and used it as a shield against the stinging drifts.

Winter brought on these huge swells: big lows that they tracked on TV until they slammed up against the coast. If the storm was far enough offshore and the wind and direction were right, Goog, Castro and Aldo would surf razor-edged lines until the dark and cold forced them home.

Of course it wasn't always like that. It could blow onshore for weeks, cold southerlies dredging up Antarctic air, sweeping the ocean flat. Huge storm swells could destroy the epic banks they had surfed all summer, sucking up the sand and closing out along the beaches. The winds scoured the beach carparks, sand blasting rusted old wagons where surfers waited for a lull or a miracle. Sooner or later they turned their cars around and headed for the video shop to rent the latest offering from Fiji or Indonesia. They would pull bongs and dream of warm water. Goog hated the waiting; he hated winter.

The others came in. Castro was first, bellyboarding his way into the shorey like a kook with his arms out and mouth open. Aldo waited for a set, although it was hard to make anything of the mess the wind had left. He flat-palmed the water in anger. Goog could see his head tilted back as he shouted at the sky. He could imagine Aldo's savage *fucks*, his teeth-clenched curses, as if the ocean had something personal against him. Eventually Aldo caught one, a shitful three-footer with no wall, just the lumpy roll of a sea-monster's head. Castro waited for him at the water's edge; some loyalty had formed in those last minutes of the session. That was the rule of three – one always had to miss out. They came up the beach together, their hands describing bottom turns and reos.

Goog watched them walk towards him: Castro, long and thin as a water bird, keen brown eyes darting back to the water; Aldo, short and square as a box, scuffing the sand with his feet.

Aldo opened his mouth and let go with the usual crap. 'What happened to you, ya poof?'

Goog held up the halves of his board.

'That's a poof's excuse.' Aldo looked to Castro for approval but he was pulling at his wiry little goatee with his fingers and looking out to sea, to the gathering heads of whitecaps and the foul grey horizon.

'Indo, guys, is going off as we speak. Cold Bintangs, luscious Balinese babes, palm trees. Think about it. G-land at full

ater barrels at Lakey Peak, dropping into the
It'd be huge.' Castro always turned to Indo
nore and winter made him worse. He was an
reak. His room was covered in maps and travel posters;
shadow puppets dangled from his roof.

'Yeah, I bet those Indo chicks would love a bit of this.' Aldo
put a fat paw on his gonads and gave them a good shake.

'What makes you think they'd be interested in you, you
wanker?' Goog hated it when Aldo went on like this. He
couldn't help thinking of Marcella – Marcella and that dirty
bastard with his hand on his dick.

'Okay, poofhole, you wanna make somethin of it.' Aldo
pushed him hard in the chest 'You know what your trouble is,
you're an arse-bandit. That's it, isn't it!' He shoved again and
Goog fell back in the sand.

'He's got a girlfriend, Aldo.' This wasn't news to Aldo.
Castro was just trying to calm things down.

'Shit, call that a girlfriend. More like a fucken whippet on
heat.' Aldo talked big about women but he hated them. He
hated most of everything. He hadn't wanted Marcella; she
hadn't wanted him. It wasn't even the sex, Marcella had said
later. She had done it to get back at Goog, to make him pay
attention. She had done it to stop him being *Mr Fucking
Complacent*. Those were the words she used.

Goog lay back in the sand, his anger boiling his insides dry.
Later he would think of things to say, ways to punch Aldo
so quickly he couldn't hope to defend himself. Later he would
think.

Castro raised his palms to the two of them. 'Come on,
guys, let's go and have a mung at Goog's place. Your mum's
out, isn't she?'

Goog nodded. His mum was on dayshift until the weekend. He accepted Castro's cold, salt-chapped hand.

Aldo drove back through Torquay's grey streets, his arm hanging over the wheel like a leg of lamb. Castro rode up front on the bench seat with his arm around Saxon, Aldo's dog. Despite being the ugliest dog around and belonging to Aldo, Saxon was actually a pretty mellow beast. He slobbered over Castro's arm and Castro wiped the strings carefully onto the seat.

'Easy with the fucken car, mate.'

'Hey, it's your dog's slobber, buddy. Anyway, it's not exactly a bloody Beemer, is it?'

Aldo brought his teeth together and swore at the road. They drove past Rip Curl, with its specials on two-mill springies and board shorts, past the shuttered factory outlets and summer cafes with rubbish in their doorways, up Goog's street – a silent valley of peeling weatherboards and brick veneers, soon to be pulled down and replaced with pastel-toned hardiplank and glass for the weekend blow-in latte-sipping mobile-phoners.

Aldo chucked a U-ey and pulled up in front of the three-bedroom fibro that Goog shared with his mum and younger sister, Annapriya. Dad was long gone, Goog didn't know where. Eight years ago he got a card from Kalgoorlie, and then (apart from a freak call on his eighteenth birthday) Dad had exited his life for good.

Inside, the house was freezing. It had been built when insulation was considered a luxury, so it was an oven in summer and a fridge in winter. The walls were so thin they bent when you leant against them. The ashtray was full of fag ends ringed with Mum's bright pink lipstick; a white coffee cup was stamped at the rim with the same symbol. *Mum's Breakfast Ritual* – a still-life on the coffee table.

Castro jumped the back of the couch and eased a long fart out of the fake leather. He jammed a tape into the VCR, the one he carried everywhere: *Bali High*, made in 1984 and sporting the dodgiest soundtrack ever known. Synth music was big in 1984 – that and dull American commentary. Goog zapped the sound to zero and went to get some food.

'This the new *Tracks*?' asked Castro, flipping through the magazine for anything of value.

'Yup.' Goog stood staring into the fridge like a homesick penguin.

Aldo stalked angrily around the walls looking at Goog's photos. 'What the fucken hell is this?' He pointed at a picture of a sheep's skull.

Goog had underexposed it two stops and then burnt in the skull, isolating it from the dark background. That photo had won Goog his new camera: first prize in *Focus Magazine*'s annual comp. Marcella had been rapt, said it was the start of something big. It was Marcella who'd talked him into sending it.

Aldo shook his big fat head. 'I just don't get your photos, mate. They are fair dinkum shit.'

Ignoring him, Goog pulled a loaf of Hi-Fibe from the fridge. He smeared a few slices with marge and then laid on a good base of Vegemite, thick-cut some cheese and sliced a few pickles on top. Aldo really hated pickles. He poured three glasses of milk and slipped the empty carton back into the fridge door.

'Check this out, Goog. G-land cooking at eight foot. Man, I wish I was there now.' Castro was off again.

Aldo started in. 'You're a fucken dreamer, Castro. Where

you gunna get the cash to go there? You should get a job. Both of you should, ya lazy arseholes. It's me that's supportin you bludgers.' This was an unusual tack for him. He never criticised Castro.

Castro looked up from the magazine and raised his eyebrows. 'Yeah, any jobs going at your work, dude? I must admit it's a lifelong dream of mine to stick pieces of metal together.'

'Fuck you, mate. Here, give us one of them sand-bitches.' Aldo grabbed a sandwich and stuffed the whole lot into his mouth. His jaws worked on it for a moment and then he stopped. His eyebrows drew together, steepening like a rogue-set over his eyes. Putting his fingers into his mouth, he dragged out a pickle like he was pulling a tooth.

'What the fuck is this?' He held the pickle between his finger and thumb. It flopped down like a dead mouse.

'It's a pickle, Aldo.' Goog battled with his smile.

'It's fucken wog-food, that's what it is. I only eat Aussie food. What're ya tryin to do, poison me?'

Not a bad idea, thought Goog, but he kept silent as Aldo spat the whole mess into his hand and dropped it into the ashtray with Mum's morning offerings.

Castro rattled on. 'Indo, guys. Check out the waves, all that warm water. Think of charging all day in just a rashie and boardies. Coming back to the hut for a banana smoothie and pancakes.' There was no doubt about it, Castro knew his fantasy inside and out. 'Man, think of a massage with coconut oil after three hours of screaming barrels.'

Aldo missed his cue for some smut because he had pulled out the Scrabble board and was riffling through the bag for letters. Castro dropped the magazine and went over to the stereo. Goog's Mum didn't believe in CDs, she still thought they were a passing phase and that vinyl would make a big comeback. So his family was trapped behind the heavy door of history while the modern world partied on outside. Creedence, The Doors, The Divinyls, Cold Chisel – big uncomfortable chunks of scratchy plastic that hissed and jumped every time they were played.

But Castro loved them, loved the way they felt in his hands, the artwork on the big cardboard covers, the lyrics printed on inserts or foldout panels. He loved the ceremony of putting on a record – dropping it carefully on the turntable, wiping it clear of dust as it spun around. You could see the leaders, the blank circles between the tracks. It took skill to drop the needle where you wanted it. You had to count the tracks, broad rings of grooves like asteroid belts, until you got to the one you wanted. Then down gently with the needle, soft as a moon landing.

Jimi Hendrix. *De ne ne ne Da na na na . . . De ne ne ne Da na na na . . .* Castro pulled his fingers through the chords, jumped on the couch and arched back in full air-guitar mode.

Goog sat down and looked at the cover of *Tracks*. The usual 'Is Surfing Better Than Sex?' article, one on Indonesia, page after page of competition rave and a story on south Western Australia titled 'Rhino chasers and elephant guns: The big south-west experience'. Goog flipped through to page sixty, glancing at the Reef Brazil girl on the way.

The story was about two surf-crazed groms carted by Dad halfway across the continent to experience the big waves of Margaret River. It was bullshit. What dad in his right mind would spend three weeks in a car with his teenage sons, even if there was a possibility of them being trashed by freight-train waves? But shit, what did Goog know about dads?

What got Goog were the pictures – wide panoramas of

desert with a strip of blacktop arrowed through its heart; ten-foot peaks with surfers clawing their way over the tops; camp-fires and tents. Life here seemed so complicated by comparison. The fortnightly pilgrimage to put in his form, his mum's constant questions, and the pressure from Marcella that was more than he could bear, even over an STD line from Melbourne. It was small-town suffocation, a two-minute holdown breathing sand and water while the world roared on above.

Castro lurched into view, panting from his guitar solo.

'Whatcha reading?' He dropped into the seat beside Goog and grabbed the magazine.

'Just some crap about Margaret River.'

'Any good?'

'It's crap, mate.'

'We should get out there. Pile into Aldo's Kingswood and head out west into the setting sun.'

'We're not takin my fucken car.' Aldo looked up from his solo game of Scrabble. He had made the words FUK and COOC and was trying to add up his points.

'Fuck it then, we'll skateboard. Let's do it. There's nothing going on around here. What have we got to lose? We could get jobs in Perth or up at the mines and fly up to Indo. Surf our way through the islands and then hop over to Sri Lanka. There's cranking coral reefs all round Sri Lanka. Pure filth, and ours for the taking.'

'They're in the middle of a civil war, Castro.' Goog dropped in with some reality.

'Or the Philippines. Unnamed breaks, we'd be the first there. They'd call them after us – *Castros*, *Googs*, *Knobjuice*.'

Aldo flung a useless Q tile at Castro. 'I'm *not* fucken comin. I've gotta job, ya know.'

'We'd live on the beach, gather coconuts, catch fish, learn to speak the lingo, go native.' Castro was wild and Goog felt himself sweating with the fever of his words.

'You're weird, Castro. You're crazy, man.' But Goog was laughing.

Only Aldo sat moping. Wallowing in his isolation, his arms folded, his swastika tattoo still red and scabby under the thick wires of hair and slag scalds. 'I'm not fucken goin. I'm not.' His lip, pushed out like a rock ledge, made him look like a sulky child.

Goog walked around Torquay, seeing everything for the last time. He remembered a line from an old song (a really old song, older even than Mum's stuff), something about everything you looked at seeming new again. Alice was riffling through the bins near the plaza, chanting her weird little mantras, her port-stained lips moving like startled baitfish.

'I'm off, Alice.' Goog could say whatever he liked to Alice without it having any consequence, any meaning. He liked that about her. Some days he'd just come down here and pour his heart out while she drank out of old cans and slipped newspapers under her cardigan. 'I'm leaving all this behind.' He swept his eyes over the plaza, its dark shopfronts and windblown gardens. 'This is really all I know and it scares the shit out of me to leave. But I can't stay. Castro, me, even Aldo – we've outgrown it.'

Alice looked up from her bin. 'Yesssss,' she replied nodding as the esses seeped from her mouth. She pulled a plastic bag out of the bin and held it up against the sky, looking for holes.

'theydonnowhattheythrowawaythisisgoodstuffforgive-themohyesforgivethemyup'

She blinked at the watery sun pissing through the bag.

'nothinwrongwiththisbagnonothingnothinnothin nup sagood-unthisone'

Alice sat on the pavement and spread the bag out in front of her, ironing the creases flat with her palm. Goog watched her tuck the handles neatly inside the neck of the bag and then roll the whole thing in on itself.

'cmeredownere comeoncomeon come' she said.

He crouched down to Alice's level and she gently crowned him with the plastic bag.

'keepthesunoff keepitoffyupyup' She nodded again and pulled her lips back to show the rotted stumps of her teeth.

Goog fished out a two-dollar coin and pressed it into Alice's oily palm.

'Have a cup of coffee on me,' knowing full well that if she could scrounge four dollars more she'd buy a bottle of Queen Adelaide and curl up happy for the night. They stood there for a while in silence.

Then Alice looked up at the sky and said, 'raintonight rain-rainrainrain rainyup'

Suddenly there was nothing left to say. Even the seagulls stopped their insistent screeching. Goog often felt like this, alone in the company of others. At least Alice didn't seem to notice.

'Well, I'd better make tracks, Alice. Take care, all right.'

'tracksyup tracks goooodidea tracksyup'

As he turned his back on Alice and the stinking piles of rubbish that she valued so highly, Goog swore he heard her say, 'Fear.' And then after a pause, 'Swallow your fear, boy.'

But when he looked back at her she was making paper flowers from old tissues and cooing at the sky.

2

GOING-AWAY PARTY

If Goog's mum had known about the party she would never have allowed it. She wouldn't let a bunch of drunk surfers do helicopter spews in her lounge room. But they picked a night when Goog's sister, Annapriya, was at Aunt Barb's and his mum was working. As Castro said, what she didn't know would never hurt her.

The party had been two-and-a-half weeks in the planning. Word had passed round town in the usual jungle-drum way and it was going to be huge. The preparations had been fairly standard stuff – invite everyone, buy some jumbo bags of chips and order a keg.

Bloodhound was responsible for tapping the keg. He had grown up in a pub and was an expert in the ways of beer. It was an art, he said. You needed just the right feel for it or it could go all wrong. You needed a steady hand and a keen eye, you had to be in tune with the keg, handle it like a dangerous beast. The keg could be your best friend or your worst fucking enemy. It was like defusing a bomb.

It ran pure froth for the first hour and the house was only

saved from the restless crowd by a quick mercy dash to the bottlo. Just when they'd been calmed down with VBs, someone cranked the music up a couple of notches. Unstable chips of plaster and flakes of paint vibrated from the walls and ceiling and, working their way into stubbie necks, were swilled on down. This mix of plaster and beer, far from settling the situation, made it wilder and more uncontrollable, as if by tasting the house the crew had to consume the whole thing.

Dancing was a pure contact sport. The clocking of ribs and collarbones was drowned out by Thin Lizzie and Led Zeppelin, Mum's ancient albums pushed to their fragile limits. Shoulders curved into walls, heads connected. At the edges of the room the girls dodged bodies between gulps of day-glo alcoholic lemonade and waited patiently for it all to be over. In the kitchen someone ran wild with a sauce bottle. The walls were covered in red spirals and the fridge was a piece of installation art.

The stereo needle chased the grooves, hopped flattened ridges and bounced between repeated words before the whole record was frisbeed out onto the front lawn at a speed far greater than $33^{1}/_{3}$ r.p.m. There was a growing pile of vinyl-mulch beneath the weary silky oak.

Aldo arm-wrestled Trig on the kitchen bench; Trig, the one-eyed fatman from Jan Juc. His biceps were like Christmas hams, tapering to thin wrists and delicate hands. He was sweating and grunting.

'Give up? Do ya?' Aldo was smiling, his teeth grinding slowly behind his lips.

Trig was nearly crying with the strain. 'Nuh. Nuh.'

Aldo cranked his arm over a notch. 'Come on, ya pussy, push it! I'm not even tryin here.'

A crowd began to form around them. They pointed their

stubbie necks at Trig's sweaty face and Aldo's scarred forearm with its cabled veins. Bets were laid.

In the lounge, Castro leapt onto the coffee table and whipped up a fury-dance, butts and bottle tops exploding from his heels like sparks. As the record screeched to a halt, he stretched himself up into a shaky handstand and was showered with peanuts and beer froth. The table wobbled for a moment and then began to keel over like a sinking boat. A leg creaked open at the joint and folded back. Castro fell like a sack of mussels, his shoulder ripping down through the carpet and opening a hole in the rotten floorboards.

Owler called out, 'Gangs-on!' and jumped on Castro.

A stray homie swung in from the front door and swallow-dived onto Castro and Owler. Dregs handed his stubbie to his girlfriend and joined the pile. Then Igor jumped on, followed by Jitters and a bloke from Anglesea built like a Kenworth truck. Castro was pressed flat to the carpet by six bodies, sweating alcohol and dope. The only thing that saved him was the airspace created when he broke open the floor.

Back in the kitchen Aldo was king and his subjects were chanting for him.

'Aldo! Aldo! Aldo! Aldo! Aldo . . .'

Trig was dripping sweat onto the bench, his real eye shot with so much red it looked like a road map.

'Give up now? Gawn! There's no way you can win.' Aldo looked quickly around at the faithful. They nodded.

'You're going to lose, Trig.'

'Give it up, man.'

'Throw it in, dickhead.'

But Trig was sick of losing. He tightened his grip and, whimpering, forced Aldo's arm past the halfway mark. Aldo grunted and his shoulder rose as he levered Trig's arm back to upright. He smiled as he pushed it slowly towards the bench, further and further back until Trig's shoulder looked like it would pop from its socket. With a final grunt Aldo slammed Trig's arm down, bursting his knuckles on a pile of beer nuts.

The crowd exploded. Tomato sauce flew through the air like streamers, beer rose in champagne-like fountains. Aldo was handed a couple of stubbies and, plugging one in each corner of his mouth, he drained them. The crew cheered and slapped him on the back. Two freshies appeared.

Aldo looked at Trig, his forehead flat on the bench. 'What a fucken loser,' he said.

Goog lay in his bedroom with Marcella, trying to ignore the carnage beyond the door, trying to concentrate on this moment because tomorrow he would be gone and this would be his only memory. She had caught the train down from Melbourne to share his last night in Torquay. She had lit candles in his room and unwrapped an oil burner from a length of silk. The room was full of waxy black smoke and patchouli fumes.

Marcella propped herself up on an elbow, turning her hair through her hands like worry beads.

'What is going on here, Goog? I kept my half of the bargain. I'm going to uni and here you are going for Dickhead of the Month with your fucked-up no-hoper mates. If there were prizes for Most Unmotivated, you'd win them all.'

Goog pinched a stray loop of hair and brought it to his nose. He brushed his nostrils with it, smelling shampoo – musk or lemon, he couldn't decide. Why did Marcella always have to push him? Couldn't she just relax and let it happen? All this talk of the future made Goog nervous. The future would be here soon enough and then he would deal with it.

Outside in party-land, gatecrashers had locked themselves in the bathroom and were sharing joints in the bath. Desperately full drinkers were beginning to piss on Goog's mum's lavender hedge. The smell of lavender and urine blew in through the front door. In the bedroom patchouli was the order of the day. The oil was burning and Goog fought the urge to cough.

Marcella started up again. 'It's not too late to give up this stupid trip with the unDynamic Duo. There's still the mid-year photography intake. You could try and work on your folio. You'll be a year behind me but that's still cool, I could wait for that. I'm just not going to wait around for nothing.'

'Jammer . . . Jammer . . . Jammer . . . Jammer . . . Ja —' The noise from the lounge room was battering against Goog's door, beer was beginning to leak under it. The smell of candle wax and patchouli fumes had claimed the air inside and pushed Goog under his doona. It was dark under there, and full of Marcella's smell. Goog breathed the warm air and wondered if he loved Marcella or just the thought of her. He had created this image in his head, a mental photo, which was easier to deal with than the real person.

'What are you doing, Goog? Come out from under there, talk to me!' She pulled the tip of his ear until he was back in candle-land. 'What are you even going for? What have Castro and Aldo got that I don't, apart from an understanding of board geometry and the ability to use a mull-o-matic? A month away and what then? You get home and what's changed?' Marcella's dark-brown irises shivered. They did this when she was angry or upset. Goog found it difficult to look at her, at those eyes, when it happened.

'Look at me!' she yelled. 'What then, Mr Motivation? You think you can be like this forever? It's not going to happen, Goog. Everyone will leave you behind, even your mates will grow up – one day.'

Her wobbly eyes began to leak. Goog brushed at the tears with the ends of her hair. He was sure he loved her in these moments when she was softer and easier going. This was the side of her he wanted. This new phase they were going through, this serious stage, was too much. He swept the ends of her hair over her face, painting her cheeks with her tears.

In party-land a chair was exiting a window and someone was eating one of Priya's goldfish. Marcella knocked Goog's hand away, reclaimed her hair and began to chew it as she talked.

'I'm going to be a writer. And while you're busy *talking the talk* I'll be out *walking my walk*. I'll be walking towards my dream.' She stared hard at Goog. Only he and Marcella were in the room, but she had a writer's need for emphasis. 'I'm going to become a writer, *then* I'll travel – Asia, Europe, America. I'll still live by travel writing but I'll just have to find another photographer along the way.'

Goog tried to kiss her but she moved her head so that he grazed her long, straight jawbone with his lips. This wasn't going exactly as he had planned. There should have been a lot less talking, none of this arguing.

'It could have been you, Goog. You and me – a team. What is it with you? Is this what you want?' She stabbed her hand like a sword at the corners of the room to indicate the life he could expect. The smoke parted for a moment and Goog could see her eyes shiver in what remained of the candlelight. She shut them and, dropping off her elbow, covered her face in her thick hair.

She was silent for a long time. Then she said, 'Come on,

Goog,' and leant over him and sucked in his bottom lip. Her eyes were open, looking straight into his. This was better. This was much better. Her tongue ran along his teeth, slid into his mouth. As he reached up for her, she pulled away. 'Come on, Goog. Come up to Melbourne. We can be together. You've got talent, everyone says so. Once you get your degree and I have mine we'll take that trip. Together we'll be the best —'

The door crashed open. 'What're you doin, ya poof? Aren't ya havin a beer?' It was Aldo framed by the doorway, swaying like a shallow-rooted tree.

'Piss off, Aldo.' Marcella's eyes were on the wobble again. She threw a pillow towards him but Aldo managed to deflect it with his face.

'Was I talkin to you, bitch-features? Was I? Why'nt you come over here and make me piss off? Come on —' And then a stray gust of patchouli caught him off guard and he swung down to the floor with his heels as a pivot. The Gangs-on Gang spotted him and lumbered into action.

Marcella got off the bed and gave Goog a light kiss on the cheek. She said, 'Send me a postcard. And if you ever manage to get your shit together, then call me.'

She smoothed her jeans and stepped over the nasty coiling mass of the Gangs-on Gang. Goog looked out through the door to where Castro was dancing nude with a bunch of lit sparklers poking out of his arse.

The house was a write-off. Goog cleared the cans and bottles and trowelled most of the puke off the floor. He unblocked the toilet with the mop and set the fridge upright. The carpet had deep scorch marks from cigarettes and sparklers. One wall had three fist marks in it where a Jackie Chan demonstration had gone wrong. Someone had turned the water off at the mains. The bathroom sink had been wrenched off the wall and the now three-legged coffee table was smouldering on the front lawn.

At least his new board had been spared. He pulled his hands down the smooth rails and spun it over to admire his name pencilled in beside the stringer. Goog's mum had donated four hundred bucks from her holiday jar. He'd had to tell her you couldn't even get a decent second-hander for that – it was short about two hundred. She'd cut the groceries back that week, didn't pay the gas or phone. Priya went without a new uniform. She'd eventually handed him six hundred and told him to make sure he got his money's worth.

Whose board was it, anyway? Was this one of those conditional presents? Was he supposed to be full of gratitude and respect for Mum's sacrifice? She was always doing things like that – giving up, doing without. She loved to play the martyr.

Goog remembered how his footprints had looked in the dust on Wayne's concrete path the day he'd walked over with the money burning a hole in his pocket.

He could picture the lone lemon tree in the backyard, like something from a snow-dome. Wayne worked out of a fibro shack round the back of his house, and there was always a cloud of foam dust in the air. He had put in an exhaust fan only last summer. Before that he'd tied a rag around his face and brought up smooth white phlegm-balls in the middle of sentences. Not that he ever had that much to say, unless he was raving on about board design. Goog rarely saw him out in the line-up. He usually woke in the dark and chased the big southerly swells that rammed the other side of Cape Otway.

Goog bounced his knuckles off the flaking wooden door and peered in through a window. It was frosted over with dust. All he could make out was a dark shape swaying like kelp under the fluorescent light. He could hear the low drone of the fan and the annoying whine of a planer, so he invited himself inside.

Wayne was planing down a blank, running his hand over the deck and sighting along the rails for imperfections. The walls were lined with board templates and curled photos. Goog had a closer look at the photos. The emulsion was burnt with age and exposure to acetone, light and resin, but Goog could see the waves. Big waves. Below them, in biro, someone had recorded the date and the place. *Todos Santos 1976*, *Grajagan 1984*, *Cactus 82*. And then one that had made Goog's heart skip a beat: *Margaret River 1971*.

It was an awesome wedge of a wave, thick-lipped and mean, with chop on the face like ski jumps. The surfer was under-gunned, the nose of his board had lifted up and his arms were flung out wide like wings. It was taken from the shore, so Goog couldn't see his face but he could imagine it – mouth and eyes round; pupils pinprick small; nose flared wide, breathing fear. He had taken the drop and was fully committed. Goog could see air under the nose of the board, the lip feathering in front of him and plumes of white water billowing like cloud at his back.

'Pretty big, huh?'

Goog snapped his head around to see Wayne pulling up his mask and resting it on his head.

'Just about bloody killed me, that one. She was a mean little beast.'

Little, thought Goog. *It would have to be fifteen foot, easy.*

'Bad choice of board. Snapped my seven-six the day before

and had to swim for it. That was all I had left in my quiver.' He stabbed his finger onto the photo, smearing off some of the foam dust. The board and surfer stood out as if they had been highlighted.

Goog felt something popping in his stomach, like it was him out there with all that water.

'I need a new board,' he said, holding Wayne's gaze for an uncomfortable moment.

Wayne pursed his lips and looked up and down Goog's body, as if sizing him up for a coffin. 'D'you snap your last one?'

'Yeah. Plus I'm going on a trip.'

Goog's eyes wandered back to the photo. Wayne moved over to the racks and laid his hand on a board.

'I got a couple here I can let you have for cheap. Good boards. Custom jobs that no one picked up.'

'I was looking for my own custom job.'

Goog watched Wayne turn round slowly and pinch his watery eyes. 'Where you going?'

'West.'

'How far west? Warrnambool? Yorke Peninsula? Cactus?'

'Further than that.' Goog pointed his chin to the photo on the wall. 'Margarets.'

Wayne ruffled some foam dust from his hair and looked at Goog while the clock above his head made a slow half minute.

'You'll be needing something a little bit special then. Taking more than one board?'

'I've only got the money for one. One good one.'

'You'll need something that's good all round. You'll miss out on the bigger days and you'll be over-gunned on the pissy little days. I guess you'll learn to live with it. I'd be taking a quiver myself.'

Wayne pulled the mask over his head and reached up for a sketchpad from the shelf. 'I'm not going to make you a rhino chaser to surf the Jan Juc shorey,' he said.

He sketched a few profiles on bits of paper and wrote Goog's weight and height beside them. Apparently he had seen Goog surf once or twice and picked his style and wave preference from that alone. Wayne was often called arrogant behind his back.

'You after decals?' he asked. Goog shook his head and a light halo of dust rose from his hair. 'Good, coz I wouldn't put the bloody things on anyway. They mess up the lines of the board. This one's okay, though.'

He flicked a logo the size of a lens cap at Goog. Goog flipped it over and saw the head of a rhino rendered in black and white, with *Wayne Schramm Designs* underneath it.

'I'm not making you a wafer, you know. Not something that you'll crease up the glass on your first drop. If you want that, there's the commercial joints in the plaza. You need a board of consequence, not some trendy little slice of pro-circuit hype.'

Goog had picked up his board two weeks later. Wayne pulled it off the rack and handed it to him. It was sleek, perfect, with just a touch of the gun about its lines. It was Goog's board, made for him alone. No one would be able to ride it like him.

'Enjoy,' Wayne had shouted at Goog's back as he'd brushed past the snow-covered lemon tree, the board tucked high under his armpit.

Goog brought his mind back to after-party damage control and laid his precious stick against the wall. He stepped over Castro, who was clutching his head so that his brain didn't leak out of his ears. Aldo was asleep where he had fallen last night, snuggled up in his own vomit. Goog wandered around in slow circles, picking up shreds of his mum's coffee-table books and chips of black vinyl. It was a meaningless act but it was slow and rhythmic and it gave him some comfort.

Then Mum appeared at the door with Annapriya. She walked inside with a faint downturn in her mouth and an alarming amount of white around her irises.

Annapriya spoke first, 'You are in soooo much trouble.'

Mum took in the devastation. There was something cyclonic about it. She picked up half an Alice Cooper album. 'Oh, Googsy,' she said. 'Why did you have to go and do this?'

That shitted Goog off more than anything, the way Mum made him feel like a child.

'It wasn't me,' he said, and then realised how stupid it sounded.

'Why, Goog? I've always tried my best for you. I've given you everything I could and you reward me with this.' She dropped Alice Cooper onto the floor. 'I thought this trip might give you something, make you grow up and work out what you want from life. But when I see this,' she offered her flat palms to the destroyed room, 'I think that maybe you'll never give anything back to the world, that you can only take.'

Priya sneered at him. 'Yeah, Goog. You're so selfish.'

'Shut up, Priya,' snapped Goog.

'Go and put your stuff in your room, Priya, this is between me and your brother.'

'But Mum —'

Mum pointed to Priya's room. A room where three people were sleeping, one of them in her toy box.

'I want this cleaned up, Goog, and then I want you to leave. It's time you took a little responsibility for your own actions.'

There was nothing to say to this. There were no smart-arse answers. Goog's mouth was full of fuzz and his brain ached.

'Sorry, Mum,' he said. But it wasn't enough. Not this time.

They couldn't leave that day. Aldo tried to drive but he barked his breakfast all over the dashboard before they had cleared town. No one else was allowed in Aldo's seat, so they were stuck.

Goog spent the night at Castro's place. His dad was up the coast on a delivery and they had the house to themselves. Castro was too hung over and Goog too ashamed to call anyone, so they spent their last night in Torquay alone, without ceremony. Goog slept on the floor beneath faded travel posters and the shadows of Balinese kites. He woke with the cat kneading his chest. At first light they crept out of town like defeated dogs, tails rammed home between their crotches.

Goog's mum was waiting for them at the roundabout on the way out. She had run her little red Corolla up onto the grass and was leaning against the bonnet, smoking a cigarette. It looked like she had been there for a while. There was a circle of butts stomped in around her feet, like the grunge-fairy had conjured up a ring. Aldo slowed down and pulled up beside her. He avoided looking at her, not really remembering his part in the destruction of her house. Castro smiled and gave her a wave. Even in her dark mood she couldn't resist giving him a small smile in return, a weary little shake of her head.

Goog got out of the car and walked over to her. She took one last drag on her cigarette and, reaching inside the Corolla, ground it into the ashtray. She pulled out an envelope.

'If you want to come home at any time, that's okay. You

know that, don't you? I haven't forgiven you for the party but you're still my son. I want the best for you, that's all.'

Goog nodded. He knew something big should be said at partings but he was all seized up inside. Mum gave him the envelope and kissed him on the cheek. He could smell the smoke and musky perfume. He could feel the waxy pink mark pressed on him like a seal.

'Seeya, Mum. Say g'bye to Priya for me.'

'Take care, okay. Take care.'

He nodded and walked away. Aldo was revving the car, blatting clouds of smoke into the air. Goog opened the door and got in. Aldo dropped the clutch and the thick smell of burning rubber filled him. Mum was mouthing something, trying to be heard over the screaming tyres. But they were away, up the hill towards Jan Juc. Running westward.

Goog turned the envelope over and lifted the flap. Inside was a ten-dollar phone card with a picture of a sun-smacked tube wrapping over a surfer. In the top left-hand corner it said: *classic margaret river w.a.*

3

GREAT OCEAN ROAD

Aldo drove with a cigarette in his mouth, the thin wisps of smoke curling into his eyes, so that they watered and he had to blink to clear them. He drove with his fat paw dripping over the wheel like melted plastic and his foot bouncing on the juice. Aldo liked to hug the centre line, swerving over to get a better view of the oncoming traffic. Goog fought down his sharp gulps for air – his almost-cries – that fed Aldo's hunger for control.

From the passenger seat, Castro was watching the water, the calm of it far out, the slow rearing as it neared the land and the savage outburst as it hit the shallows. Goog looked at his profile – the way the thin light ran down from the bridge of his nose to his chin. Castro would do something big one day. He seemed to be waiting, storing power.

The vents in the HQ were jammed full open, so it was as cold inside the car as outside. A light mist began to smear the windscreen; Aldo switched the wipers on and then cranked the stereo up to kill the slow, insistent slapping.

Goog lay across the back seat and looked up at the long tears in the roof's vinyl. He tried to conjure up Marcella's face.

They had taken Polaroids of each other, the last time they'd spent a day together. She was wearing her thick winter coat, her cheeks were pink, her thick hair crazy with the wind. Everything perfect.

He had found the photo yesterday. Marcella's oil burner had melted the emulsion so that her features were distorted, pulled at odd angles. Goog had binned the picture and packed his bags.

Aldo hit the steering wheel in time to the music – some fascist neo-nazi crap in grunty German.

'How about some new music?' Goog shouted into the front.

Castro nodded and pulled at the ockie strap holding the glovebox shut. Aldo's left hand came down on top of Castro's, his cigarette smouldering at the filter.

'This is my car and this is my music. If you don't like it then you can fucken walk all the way to Margaret River.'

Castro looked back at Goog and raised his eyebrows. If it wasn't for the rain, Goog would have got out and walked. That and the fact there were no rewards for turning back. Goog looked at the folds of fat on Aldo's neck where it rose like a swollen corpse from his collar. God, he hated the bastard. His death-metal shirt was threaded with short, white hairs – Saxon's short, white hairs. Goog hadn't even realised the dog wasn't there until now. He usually went everywhere with Aldo.

'What did you do with Saxon, Aldo?' he asked.

'Left him with my brother-in-law.'

Goog thought he saw a slight snagging at the corner of Aldo's mouth, a small downturning that could have been caused by the light or a bump in the road. Saxon's nose marks were stamped on the windscreen in front of Castro; his hair was wafting out of the air vents.

'Pain in the arse, anyway. Not much of a dog. No aggro. Fucken useless.'

Aldo's eyes began to water and he wiped them on his shirt. 'Bloody smoke,' he said and threw his cigarette out the window.

Goog was onto something here, he knew it. 'So what if we don't come back for a while?'

'I'm comin straight fucken back. I'm not hangin around no shithole town in the middle of fucken nowhere, doin nothin. I'm comin straight home. That's the trouble with youse blokes, you've got no bloody responsibility. Fucken no-hopers.' Aldo started to slam the wheel with the palm of his hand. 'You guys don't know what home is. Or family. You don't know what it is to belong.'

Aldo was losing it, Goog didn't know why.

'And you, Goog, you're a fucken idiot.' Aldo turned into the back seat, still doing eighty, the Kingswood rocking its way over the white line. 'You are an A-grade fucken idiot.'

He wanted to respond but something in Aldo's tone, the white flecks of spittle that had started to form in the corners of his mouth, kept him silent.

Finally, Castro came in. 'Calm down, Aldo. Just calm it. It's okay.'

Aldo had gone apeshit but Castro's words worked.

'I'm comin back to Torquay,' he said in a quiet voice. 'I'm comin back.'

After Aireys Inlet, they drove under the wooden arch that marked the beginning of the Great Ocean Road. The arch was cobbled together from peeled logs coated in creosote. The uprights were rammed into stone piers. It looked like something a child might make if they'd been left alone for too long with a packet of drinking straws and a knob of brown plasticine.

Goog's dad had made a big deal of the five plaques at the bottom of the arch. Mum said it was because of Vietnam, that the arch reminded him of the war, the one he fought every day. Dad had never talked about it. He'd kept a shoebox of old photos under his bed, colours so bad they made Goog wince, even back then. In them, Dad had tight smooth skin. Photos in bars and in front of torn green tents, Dad drinking beer out of tall bottles with gold labels and smiling wildly. It didn't look that bad, but it turned him quiet when Goog asked about it. There were other photos, photos that Dad kept buried deepest. Photos with the heads burnt into holes by the glowing tip of a cigarette. Names he never, ever mentioned, as if they might curse him from their shallow graves.

Dad had loved that arch, though. He'd stared at those bronze plaques for hours while the traffic flew by. The one at the bottom said: *This timber arch was rebuilt following its destruction by fire on Ash Wednesday, 16th February 1983.* Goog could remember it all, every single word seared into his brain.

Even before the fire, the arch had been replaced. Wood wasn't the best material for a memorial. It was the food of choice for so many things – termites, water, fire. But the road itself was the real monument, built by busted-up men returning from what the plaque called *the Great War*. Dad used to laugh about this. 'There's nothing great about war,' he would say and look out to sea for a moment while Goog ran his fingers over the bronze words.

The Great Ocean Road had been blasted from the cliffs, lev-
elled and graded. Much later they tarred it, widened the corners
and made it safe. Goog liked to think about the road before the
blacktop, its surface gummed with mud, sucking at the narrow
treads of ancient cars. He liked to think about the trip being a
dangerous one, the possibility of sliding off the cliffs and down
to rocks and sea. People came looking for that even now –
superbikes leaning hard into the turns, sports cars trailing
expensive cologne and the stench of hot brakes. But the danger
was gone, the last of it carried off with steam shovels and
trucks.

Dad was gone too. All Goog had was a mangy old postcard
in his duffle bag: *Kalgoorlie circa 1991*.

Between Anglesea and Lorne, where the road started to bite
into the cliff, there was a nasty flapping sound from the rear of
the car. Aldo pulled over and got out to investigate. Goog and
Castro sat inside, quietly hoping for a better omen round the
next bend. A couple of sharp blows rocked the car and Goog
turned to see Aldo flinging rocks towards the sea and shouting.
The knuckle of his right hand was dripping blood. Goog
opened the door slowly and looked towards the rear of the car.
There was an angled dent above the fuel cap; the rear tyre was
ripped open.

He stepped out cautiously. Aldo was, by this time, a little
way down the road, smoking like a volcano. The tread had
peeled back to reveal the steel belts, scrubbed clean of rubber
by the road. Goog could make out individual wires running at
an angle across the tyre. Castro's dad always talked of tyre carcasses. It was his obsession – a truckie's obsession. This tyre

was ripped open like a corpse, like a roadkill. The top belt had begun to fray and separate, revealing another underneath, a muscle diagram in a high-school anatomy poster.

Goog gave the tyre a little nudge with his toe and pulled the jack out from the under the seat. Castro was stretching his legs down the road.

Aldo stomped back. 'What are you doin, dickbreath?'

'I'm changing the tyre.'

'You are fucken not, wankdick. Give that to me!' Aldo grabbed the jack and wheel brace from Goog and set to work.

As he was cranking the car up, a truck pulled up with a hiss of air brakes, and the passenger door flew open. A backpack shot onto the roadside and rolled towards the cliff. Castro stopped it with his foot.

A tall thin man swung out of the truck, long fingers on the grab rails. His hair was thick and matted and he had a beard that could hold the odd mouse's or bird's nest without any trouble. He was dirty; he was mostly dirt, his clothes full of holes and oil stains.

'Yes, and you can just bite the big one,' he said. 'I'll remember this. I am not without friends, you know!' The truck was already turning over gravel. The stranger picked up a stick and flung it at the cab, but it rattled off and dropped to the road without even chipping the paint. Then he held out his hand for the backpack.

'Thank you,' he said to Castro.

Castro watched the man shoulder the pack and walk off. When he reached the back of Aldo's car he stopped, rubbed a circle of grime from the rear window and smiled. In the centre of this cleared circle was a small red-and-black sticker – a swastika and a fist, one of Aldo's bands, no doubt.

The man walked up to Aldo, who was crouched in the mud and gravel, swearing at the wheel brace.

'Morning, *brother*,' said the man to the back of Aldo's shaved head.

Aldo looked round but, instead of replying, squinted up at him and rubbed a long stripe of bearing grease onto his jeans.

'I assume we are going the same way.' The man placed his spidery hands on the roof of the car.

Aldo spun on a wheel nut, 'I don't think so, mate.'

'I think we are on the same path, though, *brother*. Yes, I'm pretty sure we're on the same trip.' The man scratched the rough hair on his throat and looked beyond the fringe of she-oaks to the sea.

'Mate, I don't know you from a bar of soap. I don't give a fuck what kind of psycho trip you're on. I just want you to piss off and let me change this tyre.'

Castro wandered up. 'Hey, man. My name's Castro, this is Goog, and Mr Friendly, as we like to call him, is Aldo.'

The man held out his thin, tapering fingers. 'Jasper. Pleased to meet you.'

Castro took the hand. 'Good to meet you, too.'

The man held onto Castro's hand. 'I need a lift.'

Castro looked uncomfortable but he didn't pull away, 'Yeah, where to?'

'Where are you going?' He had incredibly piercing eyes, his grip was tight.

Aldo stopped spinning nuts on. 'We're not giving him a lift. No fucken way.' He talked as if the guy wasn't even there.

'Adelaide. We're going to Adelaide,' Goog blurted out.

'Brilliant, that's where I'm heading, so it looks like we are travelling together.'

Aldo grunted and spat a nasty looking oyster at the ground. 'No fucken way! No! And when I say no, I mean no! No way known am I letting this dero into my car.' He was shaking his head, banging the wheel brace on the ground.

But Jasper's pack was already on the back seat. 'This will be great, guys.' He jumped in beside his pack and the car rocked unsteadily on the jack.

Aldo let the car down, fully tightened the wheel nuts and got in. 'What the fuck is goin on here?' he said to Castro as he opened the passenger door, 'Did this dero just bludge a ride without my say so?'

Goog slipped in the back seat beside Jasper and pulled out his camera. He toyed with the aperture control and pointed it out to sea.

'What is goin on? Answer me,' Aldo said to Castro.

'Just shut up and drive, Aldo,' Castro said as he buckled up.

'Unbe-fucken-lievable. I do not fucken believe what just happened.' Aldo started the engine, stomped on the pedal and pushed the car back up to eighty.

Jasper offered Goog a cracked palm. His grip was tight; his fingers so long they circled Goog's hand. 'How do you do,' he said, and stared right into Goog's eyes. Beneath the dirt and hair the hitcher was a lot younger than he looked. It was the eyes that gave him away – the lack of crow's feet, the purity of the whites, sharp black pupils. In Australia your eyes were stuffed by forty, too much sun, too much salt water.

Now he was close, Goog could smell his rank, stale sweat.

Castro turned round and hung his arm over the headrest. He was relaxed with the barrier of the seat between them. 'So, what are you going to Adelaide for?'

'Oh, just a little business.' Jasper dropped Goog's hand.

'Look, my apologies for seeming a little desperate before. I've been on the road for days and I need to get to Adelaide, pronto.'

Castro nodded. 'Yeah, Aldo does too. Some business he won't talk about. Some little secret.' He shook his head.

Aldo reached down and cranked the stereo up until the windows began to rattle. Castro ran his hand backwards through his hair and gritted his teeth until it looked as if they would snap. He turned around slowly, very slowly, and ejected the tape.

Goog watched the tips of Aldo's ears turn purple. Then he heard the thrum of the window dropping and a small rattle as something plastic hit the road. He turned and saw a thin brown ribbon spooling over the tar.

Aldo's eyes shot to the rear-view mirror. 'That was my tape, arsewipe.'

'I'll buy you a new one in Adelaide,' said Castro.

'The fuck you will! That was a fucken limited edition Wünderkind, imported, cost me thirty bucks.' Aldo flung his half-smoked cigarette out of the window.

'Looks like it just became a little more limited,' Jasper said.

Castro's fingers tapped nervously on the back of the seat.

Aldo said, 'Listen, mate, just stay out of this, awright. Or I'll fucken toss you out now. This is my car and you play by my rules.'

'Fair call.' Jasper nodded, but Goog could see it wasn't a retreat. Deprived of an argument, Aldo lit another smoke and pushed the car up to ninety.

'So where you from?' Castro eased back into conversation.

'All over. A soldier of fortune, you might say. I've been travelling since I was fourteen. Working a bit here and there.

Smuggling when I had to. Running stuff across borders.'

'What kind of stuff? What borders?' Castro was nearly in the back seat now. Goog could see his hunger for the words and the world outside Torquay.

Jasper laced his fingers together and cracked his knuckles loudly. 'My speciality was human cargo. People without histories, people who required new histories, people who needed to be removed from history. Brigands and badmashes mostly.'

Castro looked confused so Jasper continued. 'Outlaws. People who needed to be somewhere else, whose situations demanded it.' His eyes connected with Castro's and stayed there for a while, allowing the information to sink in. 'Spent a year in Hanoi working as a journalist.'

For Goog, that brought back Marcella's lemony smell, the touch of her lips the night she left. 'You a writer, then?' he asked.

'No. Nothing that grand. I just ran stories down a wire, scarred my liver with local whisky and developed a taste for good opium. No, I was never a writer. But the road is a brilliant life. If you get bored with yourself, or your surroundings, you just move on and reinvent yourself.'

'Who did you write for?' Goog just couldn't leave it alone.

Castro slapped Goog's knee. 'Ease up on the writing thing, Goog.'

'Yes, and enough of me,' Jasper said. 'Where are you chaps off to?'

'Adelaide, fuckwit, we already told you.' Aldo broke back into the conversation, his eyes narrow in the rear-view mirror.

'And beyond? You seem to be set up for a big trip.' Jasper turned and patted the camping gear in the rear of the wagon.

Goog, loosened by the conversation, replied, 'Margaret River, eventually. It's a bit of a surf trip.'

Aldo swung round at Goog. 'Don't tell the dirty fucker anything.'

'You, my friend, are a little on the negative side.' There was a prickly edge to Jasper's voice.

'Mate, I don't give a rat's arse what you think of me. *This! Is! My! Fucken! Car!*' Aldo pounded the wheel for emphasis. His lips were pursed tight, his shoulders heaving and his breath coming fast through his nose.

'*And I've gotta play by your rules.* I heard.'

Goog could feel the charge in the air. He could see a big vein rising on Aldo's thick neck and his fists tight on the wheel.

Castro cut in. 'Yeah, we're off to Margaret River. After that Indonesia. Up through the islands to Java, Sumatra and then maybe we'll just hop on over to Sri Lanka and check out the waves there.' He was back in the talking chair, back with the travel brain. He was invincible, nothing could stop him.

'Ah, yes, Indonesia,' Jasper sighed, as if remembering an old friend. 'Have you heard of Nias?'

It was like asking Castro if he knew his own name. 'Sure. Full-on right-hander. Surf central – comps, guesthouses, the full ticket.'

'Well, I was there in seventy-five. Three surfers and myself discovered it.'

'Bullshit, mate.' Aldo said, 'You're bullshitting. He's bullshitting, guys, can't you even fucken see that? Open your eyes, dickheads.'

It was hard for Goog to accept that Aldo might be right but there was something weird about this guy, something that didn't add up. If Jasper was as young as he looked, then he would have been about ten in 1975.

Jasper continued, 'Yes, it was a bit of a malarial trap out

there on the point. But the waves, the way those chaps surfed them, sheer poetry. We lived off coconuts and fish. Traded all our clothes with the locals for rice and fish hooks. They surfed, I wrote. Day after day of beautiful blue sky and turquoise sea. It was paradise. Apart from the mosquitoes.'

They were coming into Lorne and Aldo drove into a service station. The oil bottles were all lined up neatly, a streamer of paper twisted over the driveway. The whole place smelled like a gas leak.

'I'm gaggin for a piss. You blokes stay here and keep an eye on this loser.' He shot Jasper a dirty look but Jasper just stared on past him to where the attendant was pumping petrol.

On the way back to the car, Aldo disappeared into the shop. Goog, Castro and Jasper sat quietly, their breath steaming up the windows. Eventually Aldo returned with three icy poles. As he got in, he handed one each to Goog and Castro.

Castro looked at him. 'Aldo, it's the middle of winter, mate. What's with the icy poles?'

'Just eat it and shut up. Fucken ingrate!'

Aldo ripped off his wrapper and chucked it out the window. Goog passed his icy pole to Jasper, who unwrapped it and took a noisy slurp. Aldo stared at Goog in the mirror, shaking his head as he pulled back onto the road, his icy pole in his mouth.

The trendy new cafes with their bright seaside decor and chalkboard prices were shut tight against the winter rain. A sleepy-looking group of tourists wandered over from the ugly pink hotel to photograph the empty beach. That hotel had grown like a tumour overnight, swelling and dominating the seaside town.

Out by the pier, a lazy swell lumbered over the reef. They passed the pine trees on the point and turned the corner that separated the old from the new. Here, on the high side of the road, the fifties motels still battled on. Their cement sheets were mottled with salt, their kikuyu lawns cropped close by the sea air. This was where fishermen and families stayed. This was where they ate poached eggs and watched the pier. This was where old times were relived day after day, until people died or moved on. One day, the developers would walk around the point and, charmed by this slice of history, call in the dozers.

As they were weaving through the bends to Cumberland River, Goog got out his camera and framed up Jasper. He felt safe behind the viewfinder, the camera a shield against the real world. He cropped the first frame close, just the eyes and the curve of his nose. The second frame, he pulled back to capture the coils of dirty hair and the sharp crease of his mouth. Goog dropped it down a stop and went for the shutter. But before he had a chance to push the button, a big hand splayed out over his lens.

'No photos, please, Goog.' Although he was licking his icy pole like a child, Jasper's voice was firm. He pulled the icy pole from his mouth and asked, 'So you chaps fancy yourselves as travellers?'

Goog said, 'This is our first trip.'

'Well, every great journey begins —'

'Fuck! The cops.' Castro spotted the blue light approaching through the rear window. Goog turned to see the car tailgating them and heard the sharp blip of the siren.

Aldo was silent as he pulled over. He rolled down his window, sucked his icy pole and waited for the policeman to arrive.

The cop swaggered up to the car. His trousers were tight and his legs were bowed like a jockey's. He was wearing a dark-blue jacket and wrap-around shades. There were flakes of pie-crust in his moustache. He squatted down uncomfortably at the front tyre. Goog could see that his trousers were so tight, his calves would never meet his thighs. Slowly, he pulled out a pencil and pushed it into what was left of the tread. He clicked his tongue and scribbled something down. Standing up, he examined the stone chips in the windscreen and then leant on the windowsill.

'Morning, sir, may I see your licence?'

'Sure, no problem.' Aldo flipped out his wallet and gave him the card.

The cop's left hand was broad and scarred. There was a deep ridge on his ring finger; his watch was gold and big as a Kingston biscuit. He gave the licence a quick once-over and handed it back. 'And who are these gentlemen?' He pointed his nose at the other three.

'Ah, these two are my friends, officer. And this guy is just a hitchhiker we picked up after Aireys.' Aldo jerked his head in Jasper's direction.

The cop sniffed and ran his tongue over the bottom of his moustache. A light fall of pie-crust drifted into the car. 'Could you step out of the car, please, sir?'

Jasper looked confused. 'But I wasn't doing anything. I was just minding my own business. I'm travelling to Adelaide and these kind chaps gave me a lift.'

The cop ripped off his shades to show Jasper his eyes.

'*Step . . . out . . . of . . . the car!*' The cop's teeth clenched and his hand moved to his gun.

Jasper swallowed the last chunk of icy pole and pushed the stick into his top pocket. He unfolded the long strap of his body and rose out of the car, staring at the cop.

The cop's nostrils flared. 'Hands on the roof.'

'Pardon?'

'*Turn around and put your hands on the roof!*'

The cop's partner, smelling trouble, leapt out of their car and strode over.

Finally, Jasper turned around so slowly that Goog thought the cop would pistol-whip him. He stretched out his fingers, like a concert pianist, and laid them on the roof. 'Victoria gets more like Queensland every day. It's outrageous.'

Cop Number One frisked Jasper, while Number Two poured the contents of Jasper's bag onto the road. His gear was soon covered in mud and bits of wet gravel. Number One turned it over a couple of times with his polished shoe.

Jasper said, 'I hope you're going to clean up that mess when you're finished.'

'Spread your legs.'

'Pardon?'

'Your legs. Spread them.' Number One pushed Jasper's legs apart and ran his hands down his thighs.

Goog couldn't believe it. It was too much like an American cop show.

'What this?' Number One had his hand on a bulge in Jasper's baggy cord trousers.

'Would you believe it's my penis?'

'Don't be smart with me, buddy. You are in a lot of trouble.'

'For what, carrying illegal genitalia?'

Number One pushed Jasper's face onto the roof of the car. Number Two looked out to sea where a container ship was buzzing the horizon.

Jasper's lip leaked blood onto the paintwork. 'This is police brutality. It's harassment and I've got three witnesses.'

'Not me, *mate,* I didn't see a thing.' Aldo was smiling.

'Pull your strides down.'

'You must be joking!'

'Do I look like a fucking comedian to you, sonny? Get those strides off before we rip them off for you.'

Number Two was still looking out to sea, tracking the slow paths of sea traffic. Jasper undid his buttons and dropped his trousers to his ankles. He wasn't wearing any underwear and he obviously hadn't washed in a while. The backs of his legs were covered in thick brown hair that looked like it was matted with wax. The skin was pocked with angry red pimples and there was a large weeping sore behind his right knee.

Number Two looked down at the road and covered his mouth and nose with his hand. Number One ripped off a packet duct-taped to Jasper's leg. A good quantity of hair came off with it. Jasper winced but he was silent. All the colour had left his face and his left eye twitched.

'What do we have here? Talcum powder? Fairy dust? Are you a fairy, mate? Hey? Is this your magic dust? Not such a smart-arse any more.' Number One pushed Jasper back against the car. 'Cuff him.' Then he poked his finger into the package and dabbed a little of powder on his tongue. Goog guessed this was for effect, because the narcs in *NYPD Blue* did it.

'You boys can go.'

Why? thought Goog, *Why do we get to go? Aren't we accessories, or accomplices? Something? Why do we get to go?*

But Aldo just pulled the old Kingswood back onto the road, spun a token amount of gravel and waved goodbye. Goog looked back at the two cops leading Jasper and his backpack to their car.

'What just went on there?' Castro was as stumped as Goog.

'Don't worry about it, mate, the fucken dero was beggin for it. Fucken smackie! Did you see all that powder? Who would have guessed, eh. Gotta be careful who you pick up. We're not in Torquay any more.'

'Yeah, but Lorne isn't exactly Sin City, Aldo.'

'You just gotta be careful. I reckon I did us all a favour.'

'Favour? What are you talking about?' Goog wasn't sure he understood where this was going.

'Don't worry about it. You blokes'll thank me one day, that's all.'

Goog and Castro stared at the ocean. Aldo lit up a smoke and stared at the road. Two good tyres hummed on the tar and the single brake light burned on and off.

'Yeah, you blokes'll definitely thank me. One day.'

4

JOHANNA

The car slid down the sandy track to Johanna, past balding fields and the big dumb faces of cattle. The Jerseys gave way to highland cows that rubbed themselves on barbed-wire fences and stared mournfully into the wind. The trees were stunted and prone, stung with salt and sculpted into giant bonsai by the brutal winds.

The campsite was empty apart from a ute and a big canvas tent that looked like something the Bush Tucker Man had left behind. Outside the tent lay a tangle of fishing rods and a big metal esky.

Fishos, thought Goog. *At least we'll have the waves to ourselves.*

Aldo swung the Kingswood around in a great circle, chewing up the grass and ending bumper-up against a star picket. He gave Castro a quick sneering grin as if to say, *I meant that!* and pushed the door open.

'Dyin for a piss,' he said as he unzipped himself and let a steaming spray of urine into the wind.

Castro bowled out of his door and ran to the top of the

flattened dunes to get a look at the ocean. Goog was still in the car, worrying the handle of the rear door. Eventually it came off in his hand and he clambered over the bench and exited through the front.

The wind was onshore and getting stuck into the waves. It was a big day though – a good six foot on the sets. Big and ugly. Goog could feel his stomach churning with the shorebreak. He let out an odd strangled fart.

Castro caught a whiff as the wind dragged the methane inland. 'Easy, man, trying to gas us or what?'

'It's big,' said Goog.

It seemed enough just to say that. The worry of going out into that mess had forced his words down inside him. Goog had surfed bigger, but these waves seemed meaner and angrier. Wayne had talked about this place, how it stuck out like a thumb into the ocean snaring all that southern juice. Goog remembered when the Easter Classic had been called off, due to six inches of nothing at Bells, and they had moved it down here, to where it was breaking at a perfect four foot. Today it was far from perfect.

Through the camera it seemed more manageable; the lens cut it into smaller chunks and allowed a bit of distance. Goog panned his lens down the beach to where two stick-figured fishos were lobbing their heavy sinkers out into the gutter. They were obviously bored. Fish hated this wind-torn water. One of the fishos began his run-up. He halted, scuffing up the sand in front of his leading foot. The tip of the rod bent back and his head turned to watch the star sinker and bait arc out into the savage water.

'Gonna suit-up?' Castro was looking at Goog with raised eyebrows, the wind dragging his hair out to one side. It wasn't even really a question, more of a challenge. The only way out was to blame the conditions and make it seem as if he wouldn't even consider wasting his talents on this shit. Castro would know but he might just let it ride.

'Nice fucken day!' Aldo walked up with piss stains on the front of his jeans and over both his runners.

'You coming out?' Castro asked Aldo.

If two of them went, then Goog would have follow. Majority rules.

Aldo turned and looked at Castro, folded his arms and smiled. 'Fucken oath, mate! Could use a little clean out. Eh, Googsy?'

'Yeah, I'm in,' said Goog.

He turned his back on the beach, walked back to the car and suited-up slowly. There was nothing to gain by hurrying, it wasn't about to get any better.

As Goog got his wettie up around his knees, Castro began *the game*, shoving Goog's shoulder. Goog regained his balance and struggled to pull his suit high enough to free his legs, but Castro pushed harder and he went over. The ground was cold and damp with sea spray. Castro rolled him, coating him in sand and dirt. The game was not to complain, only to resist and pull up the wetsuit.

Aldo finished suiting-up and joined in. This was outside the rules. With two pushers it was impossible.

'Piss off, you guys.'

'Come on, ya poof,' Aldo said, nudging him around with his foot.

Goog rolled himself into a tight little ball and Aldo began to kick him harder. Too hard.

Castro grabbed Aldo by the arm. 'Come on, let's get wet.'

It shitted Goog to have Castro rescue him but Aldo never knew when to stop.

Castro and Aldo picked up their boards and ran to the dunes. The tide was full. Mutton-bird carcasses rolled up the beach. Even the seagulls knew not to put to sea in weather like this. They stood about in a little group with their shoulders hunched like old men. Rain began to drive in from the ocean in great sheets.

Castro was first in the water and then Aldo, both paddling hard, trying to make it through the shorebreak before the next erratic set. It was at least five foot, thumping onto the sandbar. If you didn't make it beyond, there would be a painful pounding and a quick drag down the gutter to where the fishos were watching.

Goog wandered down to the beach and stood for a while, gawping at the mountains of dangerous water. He waited for a better lull, a longer lull, a safer lull. If it didn't come, then stuff it, he would just slink on back to camp and cook dinner to make up for his cowardice. Castro was making good headway, easing into a rip that was channelling back out through the messy, lunging peaks. Aldo was behind and looked like he was tiring. *Good*, thought Goog, *I hope he gets the big eat!*

And it happened like that, as if the old surf god Huey had his ear to the wind and caught Goog's wish. The two of them were almost to the safety of deeper water when a rogue one poured in.

It was five or six foot when it struck the outside bank, huge and angry, great boils appearing on its face. It jacked up to eight foot and, finding too little depth to hold its shape, threw itself forward with a boom that seemed to suck everything from the air. Far from spent, though, it began to reform over the shallow bank where Castro and Aldo were now desperately paddling.

Castro was frantic. His chest reared off his board and he tugged at the water as hard as he could. Aldo looked suddenly small and defeated.

Castro pulled up the face of the wave – six foot at least and beginning to suck sand. He punched through the back as the top began to fold downwards. Aldo wasn't so lucky. Goog could see him looking up as the wave rose to its full height – maybe eight foot. His shoulders rose as he sucked in as much air as possible. He pushed the nose of his board under as the wave drove itself at the beach. There was too little water to dive into, most of it rushing up the face, turning back round where the lip used to be and falling again like brutal rain. Only it wasn't rain, it was more like concrete.

The wave exploded. Goog could feel the sand shake, and his calf muscles trembled as the shock ran up his legs. He looked for Aldo, waiting for his board to pop back up. Nothing. Ten seconds. Twenty. Goog could hear the blood in his ears. *Don't make me go out there*, he thought. Thirty seconds. He knew Aldo's fear, his confusion, the questioning – *why me*? The waiting for it all to stop, to find the way to the surface. Forty seconds – it would feel like a lifetime under there. Aldo could probably hold his breath for a minute and a half on land, in a swimming pool, but out there . . .

Then he caught sight of Aldo's board, in one piece, way down the beach near where the fishos were standing. He still couldn't see Aldo. *Shit, don't let him die*, thought Goog. *I hate the bastard, but don't let him die. Not like this. Not because of me.* But it wasn't because of him. It was the perfect crime, he had only wished it. *Still, don't let him die.*

Castro was rising and falling on the incoming waves. He spotted something closer to shore and took off on a six-footer.

It barrelled messily and Castro tucked inside. He made it out and pulled high and over the back allowing it to blow itself onto the sandbar. Then he paddled over the bar to the gutter.

Goog could see Aldo now, floating on his back and being dragged quickly down the gutter. If he didn't liven up and swim for shore, he'd get sucked into another rip and back out into the soup. Castro was closing in on him. He caught Aldo as they drew level with the fishos, pulled him onto his board and headed towards the beach. The shorey took care of the rest, rough-handling them up to the high-tide mark, and allowing them to crawl onto the sand. Goog ran along the beach to meet them.

Castro was spun out. 'That was heavy.'

Aldo couldn't even speak. He just stared out at the ocean and shook his head, salt water draining from his nose. His legrope, still attached to his ankle, led back into the water, to the plug that had pulled free of his board. Goog looked at Aldo and noticed the tremor in his hand as he rubbed his eyes.

'Youse blokes awright?' The fishos had walked over with Aldo's board and were staring at them as if they were mad.

'Yeah, we're fine, mate. Thanks.' Goog spoke for the crew, as if somehow he were part of the heroics.

Castro looked at Goog and smiled. 'I could use a beer,' he said.

'My shout.' It was the least Goog could do.

Back at camp, while the two wetties dripped over the ringlock fence, the fishos brought them some wood and set their esky and camp chairs down. They had salt-chapped faces and big rough hands. One was tall and flabby in a beer-drinker kind of way; the other was thin and tough-looking, like a leather belt. They could have been a perfect comedy duo.

'Mind if we join youse f'r a beer?' Leatherbelt twirled a dreadlock into his goatee and looked at the three of them. There was a scar running the length of his jaw.

'No worries.' Goog made himself the host, cracking open stubbies, pouring a tin of beans into the billy. 'Do you guys want some dinner?'

'We're right, thanks.' Leatherbelt again. It was obvious that he was the spokesman. 'That was some drubbing you took out there, mate. We were pretty surprised to see you pop up again. Y'r bloody mad going out in that.'

Aldo just nodded. Goog had never seen him so quiet.

'So what're your names, anyway?' Castro squinted through the smoke at the two fishos.

'Yeah, I'm Al. Me mates call me Mullet on account of a hair-cut I once had. And that's Jim.'

'Jimbo. Call me Jimbo.' He was older than Mullet with big watery eyes and a crooked nose.

'I'm Castro and that's Goog. Aldo's the one I pulled out of the surf.' Castro gave Aldo a big not-so-innocent grin that said: *I saved your bacon, mate, you owe me one.*

'Fuck off, squidlips. I was doin okay until you came along. Could've made it back in by myself.'

'Didn't look like it from where we were standing, mate.' As Mullet grinned, his bottom jaw pushed forward and his scar stretched out like a thin rubber band. 'Looked like you were headed for the bottom.'

Aldo said nothing. Older blokes made him wary, he could never tell which way they would jump.

Mullet asked, 'So where are you three off to?'

Castro said, 'Margaret River and then maybe Perth, earn some money and fly up to Indo for a season.' He used *season* in a way that made him sound like a pro surfer.

'Going along the Bight, then. You'll see some mighty water there, fellas. Makes this look like a frikkin tea-party by comparison. We were there a couple years ago, eh, Jimbo?' Jimbo nodded his head as he sucked the dregs from his stubbie and fished another one out of the esky.

'Big Noahs too, fellas. Great Whites. I'd be buying some mesh suits in Adelaide. We fished this spot, *Ladders*, frikkin mental it was. There's these rickety old wooden ladders tacked to the cliffs. One wrong foot and . . .' He dropped his hand into a dive, whistling a thin descent. 'We pulled out some huge trevally off the rocks. I was pulling one big bugger in, putting up a hell of a fight it was. Next thing there's this tug on the line and all's I'm left with is a frikkin head. Snapped clean behind the gills it was. Saw a few guys out surfing. Remember thinking, rather them than me. Locals mostly, with beat up old cars, stinking of burning oil. Wouldn't talk to us, not even to say g'day. One day we got back to our car and the tyres were flat and there was wax all over the windscreen. Took us frikkin ages to get it off.'

Goog tried to appear cool. 'Sounds like a nice place.'

Castro leaned forward to the fire. Goog knew he was already out in the desert, climbing down those ladders, pulling into perfect barrels while bulky shadows rolled underneath him.

'Yeah, it was weird,' Mullet said, 'The desert's beautiful, though. Just sunsets and horizon and nothing in between. Loved that desert. Can't get it out of me. I cleaned the car when I got back and got a kilo of red sand from inside the doors. Got it in a jar at home to remind me.'

Aldo rolled a log over with his foot and a cloud of sparks rose up. 'How long are you guys stayin?'

'We're off tomorrow. Back to Warrnambool. Work.' Mullet shrugged as if it were a piss-poor excuse for leaving. Which it was. 'Jimbo's a brickie, I labour for him.'

Goog found it hard to picture Jimbo being the boss, telling Mullet where to stack the bricks, shouting at him when the mud was too thin or he forgot to add lime. It was hard to imagine Jimbo talking at all.

They ate the beans while Mullet and Jimbo drank steadily, tossing their empties in a pile between them. The clouds cleared and stars began to appear. The wind dropped and suddenly it seemed like the perfect night for a party.

Mullet uncovered two bottles of overproof rum and they took turns having mammoth shots of the stuff from a chipped enamel mug. Their voices became louder and louder. They woke up the sleeping cows and competed with the roar and hiss of the ocean.

Before they knew it, they were at the stage of drunkenness where singing becomes compulsory. It turned out that Jimbo sang in a choir on the weekends. Apparently Welsh pit choirs were big in Warrnambool and Jimbo was big on Welsh chorals. The rest of the crew was short on patience and voted him off the stage.

Mullet was confident and loud and knew everything from The Beatles to Green Day. But he had a voice like a poisoned cat and refused to shut up until Jimbo sat on him.

Aldo started 'Khe Sanh', but Castro wrestled him to the ground before he had a chance to drone out the first line.

And then came the stupid human tricks.

Aldo pulled a condom from his wallet and began to unwrap

it. Mullet looked nervously at Jimbo, but Goog and Castro were wise to the trick. They had seen Aldo win beers and praise in public bars from Torquay to Queenscliff. Aldo blew through his nose to clear it and poked the end of the condom into his right nostril. He sniffed hard and half the dinger disappeared. Sniffing again, it slid up as far as the rim. Gagging, Aldo reached into his throat and tweezered the end of it with his fingers. Then, with his mouth open and his eyes watering, he pulled the condom back and forward through his nostril and throat.

'That is frikkin gross, mate,' was all Mullet could say.

Goog knew Aldo's party trick was the only action the condoms would see for the whole trip. He wanted to laugh at Aldo's optimism.

Mullet could flip his eyelids up to show their shocking red insides. That looked like the all-out winner for a while.

Castro, not to be outdone, walked on his hands and drank a beer upside down.

Even Jimbo came up with something – a unique interpretation of the belly dance, for which he had more than the standard equipment.

Mullet, massaging his sore eyes, said, 'That's the frikkin eighth wonder of the world.'

'Come on, Goog, your go.' Castro was flushed from the heat of the fire and shots of rum.

'I'm right,' said Goog. He enjoyed watching but even the shots of liquid courage wouldn't make him perform in front of these strangers.

Aldo shoved his shoulder. 'Come on, ya big girl!'

'Piss off, Aldo.' He didn't want to perform.

'What're ya scared of? Come on, stop being a poofhead.

You're so fucken weak!' Aldo leant forward, his face an inch from Goog's.

Goog could feel himself begin to shake. 'Back off, Aldo,' he said slowly.

Aldo poked him in the chest. 'Weak!' he said.

Castro pulled Aldo back by the shoulder and said, 'Come on, Goog. Have a shot. What have you got to lose?'

'Yeah, come on, mate,' said Mullet 'Everyone else has had a go.'

There was no way out.

'Okay. Okay.'

Everyone was quiet. They watched carefully while Goog tucked his hair behind his ears. He cleared his throat and did the move.

Silence.

More silence.

He did it again.

Silence.

Goog's throat was dry, he felt like an idiot.

'What? What, is that it?' Mullet couldn't believe it.

Even Goog had to admit it wasn't that impressive. Ear wiggling was bullshit, next to condom snorting and fatman belly dancing.

Aldo shook his fat head. 'That is fucken crap. That is the pissest weakest thing I have ever seen in my whole entire life.'

'Shut up, Aldo,' said Castro and handed Goog the mug of rum.

'Why should I shut up? Why d'ya keep protectin him? You his mother or somethin? Let the fucken pansy stand up for himself.'

Castro opened his mouth to shoot Aldo down but Goog

stopped him. 'Leave it, Castro,' he said, and took his mug of rum into the dark.

Aldo called after him, 'Come back, ya dickweasel. Be a man for once in your life.' But soon his voice was covered by the wind and waves, smothered in the squid-ink night.

Goog woke up next to the fire, a drizzle of ash over everything. The morning was clear and cold. He stretched out his feet and heard the bell-rattle of stubbies. The fishos were gone. All that was left was a yellowed square of grass where they had pitched their tent. Aldo was asleep in the back of the car, the rear seat folded forward and the tailgate yawning open. He was on his back snoring, his socks poking out of the doona, his toes poking out of the socks.

Goog threw off the sleeping bag and dusted the ash from his hair and clothes. Swallowing deeply, he tried to regain control over his stomach. His camera was lying nearby, exposed to the elements all night. Some days it was the most important thing in his life and some days he wished it gone. It could be so heavy at times.

Picking it up, he blew the sand from it carefully and, peering through the viewfinder, pushed the shutter release half down to check the meter. It was still a beautiful piece of equipment and he loved how it felt in his hand, the way it curved into his palm. The buttons were right there, right where his fingers fell.

He must have gone a bit mad with it last night. There were only three shots left on what had been nearly a full roll. Unscrewing the flash, he slung the camera around his neck and walked towards the beach to catch the early light on the ocean.

From the top of the dune the water looked like liquid glass, the sun glancing off the sharp lips of waves. The swell had dropped overnight to a more comfortable four to five foot. The menace of yesterday – the howling wind, the terrible anger of the sea – was gone. There was still power behind the beauty though, something muscular in the way the peaks rose and thrust out at the beach.

Goog walked to the water's edge. Out beyond the lines of swell, a school of dolphins surfaced. They raced forward and were locked inside a wave as it began to break. The wall was translucent, like the impossibly turquoise water you often saw on travel documentaries. Goog looked at the wave through the lens and pressed the shutter once, twice, three times. Then nothing. The exposure window blinked at him, he was out of film. He had three slices of memory trapped on sensitive emulsion.

The dolphins flipped out of the wave as it shut down on the beach. The black arcs of their bodies were caught against the sky for a moment and then they splashed into the water. They were back out in the line-up again before he knew it. And then Goog saw Castro rising and falling on the waves, dipping his head back and pulling a great wad of water into the air. The dolphins were all around him and he was sitting there on his board like the god of it all.

He paddled for a wave and the dolphins went with him. He pulled himself up and they slid beneath him. Goog felt the camera heavy in his hand, useless, empty. It was enough to just remember this, he told himself. The wave was a long sheet of buckled glass, the sky was visible through the back of it and the dolphins were rocketing through it like sleek missiles. Castro slid over the surface, soul-arching, alive in this quick moment of connection.

And then the dolphins were gone. Out to sea. Off to another beach, their choice only limited by the distance they could swim in a day. They were surfers too, but they were always on it, never missed a swell.

Castro paddled in, not even waiting for a last wave. He caught the shorebreak up onto the beach and lay there for a while just allowing the water to wash back and forth around him. Then he looked up at Goog and smiled.

5

ELEPHANTS

After two days of good waves, they hit a lull. Castro broke out the cards, and they turned the esky upside down and dealt poker hands until dark.

That night the rain set in. While Aldo snored inside his dry car, Castro and Goog rolled against the old canvas of their op-shop tent. It had seemed so sturdy when they were putting it up – robust, tough enough to handle a hurricane. They had added the tarp as an afterthought, and now its eyes were being ripped out by the wind. The ropes they had tied so carefully were lying around in wet snakes on the ground. As the wind blew one wall towards the other, the frame flexed with an animal groan.

The tent had required some serious pre-trip research before they'd even left Torquay. Aldo had insisted on that. His car was for him and him alone, there was no sharing. It had turned into an all-day mission.

The local camping shop had three-hundred-dollar numbers for snow-camping and hiking to Everest Base Camp. The disposal store in Geelong had a flimsy nylon A-frame for forty bucks. By lunchtime they were all hungry and ready for home.

Three doors down from the disposal store was Somefin Fishy. There were pickled onions on the benchtop and a thick coat of grease over everything. There were fish souvlakis and fish dim sims, fish bites and fish cakes. If you were after fish, then this was your place.

Aldo, Castro and Goog ordered a piece of flake each and three bucks' worth of chips, and wandered outside to give their lungs a rest while their fish and potatoes were soaked in hot oil. Next door, the St Vincent de Paul op-shop had a half-price sale.

The old chook behind the counter smiled at them and then went back to crocheting something roughly the same size and shape as a fishing net. She had a neck like a bowling bag and fingers that clicked louder than her needles. Castro homed in on the collection of ancient vinyl in cardboard boxes.

'Check this out – *Peter Frampton Comes Alive*. This is a classic, man.' There were two others exactly the same, and he slid each one out of its cover and angled it up to the light, looking for scratches. 'They're in pretty good nick. Wonder what she wants for all three? Shit, look at this.' He held up a cover that looked like the Hobbit's acid nightmare. 'Uriah Heep! Man, this place is a goldmine.'

'What do you think?' Goog was pulling on a lime-green cardigan. 'Suit me?'

Aldo snorted and walked outside.

The old lady put down her knitting. 'Looks very nice on you. There are some slacks around somewhere that go with it.'

'Ah, no thanks,' Goog unbuttoned the cardigan. 'We're actually after a tent.'

'Tent?' She looked puzzled for a moment, desperately trying

to make the connection between cardigans and camping. Suddenly she focussed and said, 'We had a tent around here somewhere. Let's have a look out the back.'

As she went through a door marked *Private*, Goog shrugged at Castro. 'Couldn't hurt to have a look.'

The room was floor to ceiling coat hangers, piles of them a metre and a half deep against two walls. They pulled a huge canvas bag from beneath a pile of yellowing newspaper and lugged it out the front.

Rolling the tent down the cluttered aisle, they examined it for moth holes and tears. It was made from thick green canvas, the corners strengthened with triangles of leather. It looked as if it belonged in the desert. Goog could already picture it rising like a rock from the sand.

They bought it – twenty dollars with three Frampton albums and a jaffle iron thrown in. As they were struggling over the road with their new purchases they heard someone sing out, 'Hang loose!' And they turned to see the old lady give a wobbly little wave from the op-shop door.

Everyone was happy, except Aldo. 'That is the biggest piece of crap I have ever seen,' he said, as he shovelled cold chips into his mouth.

Now it seemed Aldo might have been right.

'Man, this tent is going to go,' Castro yelled above the screaming of guy ropes and the popping of tent pegs.

The wind was shunting in from the sea, tearing at the dunes, bringing cold air from Antarctic waters and heavy rain that smacked through the canvas. Their sleeping bags had sucked up all the water they could and were as cold and heavy as coffins.

But the rain just kept coming, creating a small lake in which the tent flapped like a crippled sail. Where the frame touched the canvas, the rain seeped in. It mustered on the roof and dropped onto Goog and Castro, or slowly trekked down the walls, where it joined the river flowing out of the door.

When the lightning started, Goog could see the bend in the poles and the frenzied flapping of canvas. He screwed his eyes shut and pretended he wasn't lying in a tent battered by wind in an exposed paddock a stone's throw from the Southern Ocean. He pictured solid walls and a soft bed.

Around this time, the frame buckled and snapped apart. The canvas, heavy with rain, dropped down on Goog and Castro and pinned them in their sleeping bags. It felt like the soggy pelt of some sad old beast. They managed to work their hands free and unzip the bags. Finally they found the door and crawled out into the rain. Castro made for the car and tried the front door but it was locked. He tried the other three and the tailgate. They were locked too. What the hell was Aldo afraid of? Castro hammered the roof.

'Aldo, wake up. Let us in.'

'Wha? Wha?' The bastard was sound asleep.

'Let us in, we're soaked. Our tent's had the richard.' They were shivering now; the rain was not easing up.

Aldo wound the window down a crack. 'Piss off. Let me get back to sleep. The rain's gettin in.' He wound the window up.

'Let us in you bastard!' Castro pounded on the window.

'Sleep in your tent. That's what you bought the fucken thing for.'

'Aldo, we haven't got a tent anymore. Now let us in or I'll break something.'

'Okay! Easy, easy.' He unlocked the front door. 'Youse are

nothin but a bunch of pussies. Scared of a little rain.'

Castro got into the car and unlocked the other side for Goog. 'Cheers, Aldo,' he managed through chattering teeth.

'And put a towel on the seat. I don't want them soakin up all that water.' Aldo pulled his doona over his head and snorted himself quickly back to sleep.

Goog and Castro dried themselves and wrestled on some dry clothes. Sleep came in small portions, before a miserable grey dawn spread like chop fat over the horizon.

The road to Port Campbell bristled with tourist signs. It was ridiculous to cram so much scenery along such a short strip. Goog grew tired of signs, stopped caring about limestone. He started to think of the signs as stitches, holding the wound of the road together. Without them, the scenery would tear itself from the continent and become a separate state, and international tourists would fork out euros to be rowed out for a photo opportunity. Boredom could do this to you, make you dream up a different world.

With a sense of duty, they followed the sign that promised *The Twelve Apostles*. The carpark was full of campervans, touring bikes and the rattle of foreign languages. Aldo parked the Kingswood between a gaggle of Harleys and a Maui van the size of a beachside toilet block. They unbuckled, stretched and scuffed their way down to the lookout. The path was fringed with pigface and Japanese tour groups in awkward holiday poses. The sky had thrown on its blue coat and, best of all, the swell was back.

At the boardwalk they gawked at the huge chunks of stone rising up from the ocean. The signs had guaranteed *twelve* apostles but no matter how many times Goog counted, he could find only six, seven if he counted the small chunk near the beach. Once a part of the mainland, the rock had been carved into Easter Island statues by endless wave action. Today the slap and hiss of the sea was cut with camera noises – shutters and motor drives, click-whirr, click-whirr. Frame after frame.

Goog had his own camera slung around his neck, but the apostles seemed so small and lifeless through the lens. They looked like cheap postcard shots.

As Goog turned from the ocean, a German with clipped grey hair and a blue and yellow Gore-Tex handed him a camera.

'One photo, please.' He showed Goog his family – their ruffled hair and foreign smiles. 'For Hamburg,' he explained, and shrugged apologetically.

Goog looked at the camera – an impressive-looking digital.

'Only depress this button.' The man's finger touched the button. There was a beep and the image of his forearm froze in the viewfinder. He smiled sheepishly and, swinging his binoculars from his chest to his back, pressed another button that freed the trapped image. Finally, he shuffled into the group and showed his teeth to the camera.

Once behind the lens, Goog relaxed. He bunched the family together, then spread them apart. There were four of them. The man's wife had hennaed hair and quick grey eyes. Their daughter was tall and blonde, and had braces laced with bubble gum. She was fifteen or sixteen and beautiful in a bored teenage way. A second man wore a nylon jacket over a green polo shirt and had a cigarette cupped into his palm like a secret.

'My brother,' said the man, and put a big arm around his shoulder.

Goog bent down for a more interesting angle but that

obscured the two background apostles. He wanted to get this right. Memories like this should be perfect.

'Just take the fuckin thing, dicknose,' said Aldo, rocking Goog's crouched body with his foot.

Goog pushed the button. A beep, a frozen image, a slice of history held in zeros and ones inside the camera.

Castro started talking to the daughter. '*Where . . . you . . . from?*' The worst sort of pidgin English, and *loud*.

'Germany,' she replied, with enough *duh* in her voice to sink him.

Castro floated. 'In Germany, where?' Now backwards pidgin, but at least softer.

She picked at the gum in her braces. 'You know Hamburg?' Her English was flawless, with the slightest accent.

'I've *eaten* hamburgers,' Castro said. 'That any good?' And flashed his million-deutschmark smile.

It went on for a while like this, an international relationship forming, until her papa stepped between them.

'Papa!' she said, as he smiled a diplomatic smile and eased his daughter back to the safety of the family. Castro, totally unfazed by the change in audience, began to explain surfing to Papa.

'Surfing's got its rules like everything else. It's got its own structure, sorta like a government, capiche?' Castro had loosened up on the pidgin but was still dopey with language confusion. 'Okay, you got your surfers on top, your stand-ups. Then you got your kneelos, we call them cripples coz they can't even stand up, you usually find them on their knees, staring up at you like monks. Below them are your bodyboarders. Speed bumps, shark biscuits, esky lids, it doesn't matter a pinch of shit what you call them but there's one thing for sure, they're a pain in the arse. If you get my meaning.'

Papa didn't. He looked confused. He unbuttoned his Gore-Tex. It was getting warm. He looked for an escape route but Castro had him bumped-up against the railing.

'Below your speed bump is your bumstick or goatboat. Usually grey-haired old fat-bellies ride goatboats. No offence.' Castro nodded at Papa's greying hair and Papa nodded back, smiling carefully. Castro went on, 'Coz they can't paddle for shit. You see, you get a paddle like a canoe and you get to sit down. Too bloody easy, if y'ask me. Below all of them is your kook and your hodad – one's a wannabe surfer, the other hasn't even got a clue. Pretty much like you guys.'

Papa looked for his family but they had deserted him.

Then Aldo stepped up and pulled the Surf Diplomat out of the way. He began, 'The Third Reich, that's a German invention, isnit?' To Aldo, the Nazis were in the same boat as prestige cars and precision tools.

Papa looked at his white runners, rolled a pebble with his toe. That was Goog's cue to look at some limestone. He ran his camera around the cliffs and then out towards the sea. Below the feet of the stone giants, the beach curved and foamed back towards Torquay. It felt good to be on the road, to have some distance between him and home. This was a time of possibility, new beginnings. He could be free of everyone else's idea of what he should be.

Down on the beach, a surfer was running out from the base of the cliffs. He hit the water and began paddling hard into the shorebreak. There were corduroy lines running deep out to sea, set upon set of bottled thunder. The surfer duckdived again and again, snatching breaths between each wave. Punching through the final monster, he made it out the back where the sets had been breaking heavily over submerged rock. Now there was only foam, fizzing on the ocean. Sitting on his board he heli-coptered his arms, loosening out the adrenalin.

A beast of a wave began to form – big and unruly. The surfer turned and paddled into it. Two strong digs and he was up. Goog zoomed in on him. He could almost see the stoke on his face, his raw-mouthed smile.

He was drawing a tight line over the middle of the wave. As the lip began to curl, he dropped and drove hard off the bot-tom, rising up and floating over a crumbling section. The wave formed up down the line and the surfer speed-crouched as it began to feather. The lip held but the wave was steepening, sucking water upward in smooth arcs. He shifted his weight to his back foot, hands by his sides like a bullfighter, stalling his board and waiting for the tube to form. As it did, he leant for-ward again and pulled into the deepest barrel. Goog let the shutter fly. Click . . . click . . . click . . . click . . .

The surfer was fully covered by rolling water. Goog kept shooting frames. Click . . . click . . . click . . .

Tube-time could never be fully explained. The absence of outside sounds, the slowing down of time – it was like being in the centre of a cyclone. Goog envied the surfer and was glad for him; he could picture the cloudy guts of the wave and the noise like liquid wind. Being in the green room was like being underwater and being able to breathe, a full-blown miracle. Tube-riding was a religion within a religion, a moment you could tap into forever.

Click . . . click . . . And the surfer was out. He rose up to the top of the wave and kicked out as it exploded in shallow water.

'Not bad, eh?'

Goog turned to see a barefoot guy staring out at the scene. Papa was talking with Castro, trying to avoid Aldo. His daughter was bored, singing along to Yothu Yindi on her Discman and dreaming of home. Goog dropped his camera on its strap and looked at Mr Barefoot.

He was a surfer; Goog could see the fine dusting of salt on his eyebrows and unmistakable tan marks around his neck and wrists. He was wearing shorts and an old Stussy shirt without sleeves. It couldn't have been more than fifteen or sixteen degrees, despite the sunshine, but his skin was free of goosepimples. His toenails were blackened, one of them missing completely, and there was a neatly rolled cigarette behind his left ear.

Goog began slowly. 'You from around here?'

Barefoot looked at him with eyes torn by salt water. 'Port Campbell. You're not, though?'

'Torquay,' said Goog.

Picking up a pebble with his toes, Barefoot flicked it over the cliff. 'We don't get many of you fullahs this far south.'

They stared at the water for a while. A few big ones rolled in. The surfer was back in the line-up.

Barefoot asked, 'D'you get a surf in?'

'Nup. We camped for a few days at Johanna, had a couple of epic days, but our tent got blown to shit last night.'

'Yeah, nasty little squall. Deep front though, south-westerly system. Tight lines all the way off the map. Should get better than this.' Barefoot squinted out past the lines of swell to the flat grey expanse of sea.

'Did you get one?' Goog tried to mimic the cool evenness of his speech.

Barefoot nodded, 'Yup, scored a dawny at —' The name of the break was bundled off by a gust of wind. He continued, 'It was fair. Very fair, actually.'

'Where'd be a good spot for us to get one in this arvo?' This was a bold move. Goog had only known the man for minutes. There were rules that governed these things and they didn't include blabbing about local breaks to no-name blow-ins.

Barefoot looked at Goog for a while, looked back at Castro and Aldo storming the cultural barriers, and blew through the 'o' of his lips. 'Reckon *Elephants* would be goin off, if the wind doesn't get into her.'

'*Elephants*?'

'Yeah, you know – big trunk, big ears, big feet. You'd recognise him if you saw him. Reckon you might need a gun to tame this one, though.' He laughed at his own joke.

'Whereabouts is it?' Goog asked. He knew he was pushing it too far. The guy didn't know him from a lump of wax and now he was expecting directions. But he had nothing to lose.

Barefoot just looked deep into his eyes for a while, until Goog felt that he needed to turn away. He knew if he did, he would never get the location; the game would be lost. There were crusts of salt on Barefoot's eyelashes. He didn't blink for a very long time. Goog's own eyes began to water. Eventually Barefoot broke off the staring comp and said, 'Come up to the car. I'll draw you up a mud map.'

Goog went over to where Castro was trying to explain the drop-in rule to his future mother-in-law. The hand signals were flowing thick and fast. Aldo was sulking and smoking against the railing. Goog told Castro he'd be back soon and walked up to the carpark.

The guy was up at his car – a salt-battered Subaru Brumby with a matted kelpie in the back. The dog growled as Goog approached.

'Sandfly! Gerdownwithyouyabastard!' The dog immediately sat on a wagging tail and looked up at his master. The man pulled the smoke from behind his ear and lit it. Goog could see a scrap of paper in his hand with a nest of blue lines and hastily scrawled writing. It was the map. Goog wanted it so badly he had to stop himself from grabbing it.

The man scratched at Sandfly's belly. 'Don't usually give out stuff to strangers. I'm not a bloody travel info, y'know.' He drew hard on his smoke and shot a couple of smoke rings over Goog's head. 'I did a trip once. Man, did we get some juice.' He closed his eyes for a minute then said, 'Big juice and freedom. Able to pick up in the morn and move on. Surf the dawny and the arvo session and do it all again the next day.' He pursed his lips together. 'But that was years ago. Things change.' Butting his smoke on the side of the ute he folded the slip of paper once and gave it to Goog.

It was a gas bill, overdue amount $32.78. Inside the fold, danger and promises waited.

'I gotta go,' Barefoot said and swung himself into the ute. He was out of the carpark with Sandfly barking at the wind before Goog even thought to thank him.

Goog unfolded the gas bill and looked at the map. Maps were always a key to adventure – that was a lesson from childhood. They were more, much more, than directions. Maps were a window, a door, a path, a collection of lines and dots. Maps were power. He folded the gas bill carefully and went back to get the others.

The hardest part wasn't getting there, although Aldo was pissed off at the state of the track. It wasn't even following the map, which turned out to be surprisingly accurate. The hardest part of the whole thing was grubbing into wetsuits that were wet through and cold. Sodden neoprene grabbed at their thighs and shoulders. Their fingers were blue and too fat for zips. A freak offshore breeze sprang up and made them shiver.

On the map it all looked so simple. What Barefoot couldn't translate to the back of the gas bill was the heaviness of the water or the noise it made as it struck the sand. He couldn't show the distance to the break or the savagery of the waves. The map said *Long Paddle* and *Not Here, Or Here*, showing a series of crosses off the point. The crosses were rocks, sharp basalt and cupped limestone shouldering the brunt of the sea. There was an arrow pointing a safe path out through the centre of the bay, and just past the point to *Deep Water*.

Goog, Castro and Aldo stood and watched for a while. Black specks of surfers rose over the waves breaking outside the bay, beyond the left point. The break was a left-hander. This was the only thing that would work to Goog's advantage – he would be surfing on his forehand.

The whole bay was a mass of close-outs. Drifts of scummy foam blew up the beach and stuck to their wetsuits. They could feel the rumble in the sand as the shorebreak arched and buckled onto the beach.

They waited for the perfect moment, timing the sets, the short lulls between them. There seemed no end to the violence.

Eventually their moment came and they ran at the water, stroking hard as soon as they hit, paddling for the safety of deep water. The bay began to fill again. They were almost halfway out when its neck was closed off by the start of a new set. Goog reared back on his board and dug as heavily as he could with his arms. Dredging water back with his hands, he fought for deeper water.

The first wave he duckdived. The second was too big and

already breaking. Castro and Aldo were gone. He abandoned his board and, swimming down, watched the wave thrash the water above him. He rose. The waves poured into the bay, funnelled and exploded through the entrance and forced him under again. And again. He was out of breath, burnt through with cold, his head ached. There was no way he could keep this up. The coastguard would fish him out of the water a kilometre down the coast.

Then the waves stopped and the only noise was the hiss of remaining foam. He sighted Castro and Aldo further out. Gathering his remaining strength, he paddled hard. He paddled until the foam was gone and the water was black and cold beneath him.

He caught up with Castro and Aldo and they struck out for the break together. Because it was surrounded by deep water, the waves rose, broke and then petered out in isolation. Goog could see well down the coast to where the Twelve Apostles stood ankle-deep in foam, and beyond towards Cape Otway, wrapped tight in sea haze. The beach seemed a long way off, the car a dot. The point was closer but too dangerous an exit to even think about.

Castro, Goog and Aldo pulled wide of the reef and came in from the back, taking their time to breathe and set their hearts back in order.

The other surfers were sitting in a tight group in the take-off zone. There were four of them, all with long beards tipped with surfwax and thick straggly hair. There was no talk, there were no nods or smiles. This was most definitely Beard territory and they would have to play by their rules. It was no time for disrespect. This was no place for boys.

A set began to build, just the slightest rise about ten metres out. The Beards paddled out to meet it. Goog, Castro and Aldo followed like sheep, far enough back not to crowd them. They had only gone two or three metres when the wave bucked over the reef. One of the Beards gave two quick scoops and dropped vertically down its face, slotting his board under his feet as he fell. His board hit the water and he forced it onto its outside rail and to the bottom of the wave. As the wave passed underneath Goog, he turned to see it building. A rooster tail of spray came over the back and the top rail of a board appeared for a second. What had started as ten foot was now at least twelve. Goog felt his muscles drowning in adrenalin, his chest tighten with cold and fear.

The next one came in wider and slower, and the Beards let it pass. Goog was inside Castro and Aldo. One of the Beards yelled, 'Your wave!'

Goog had to paddle, he had no choice. If he paddled too slow or too weak, the wave would burn itself out without him. But Aldo and Castro, or – worse – the Beards, would pick it as cowardice and punish him. So he paddled like he meant it.

The wave began to shunt and he sprung into the crouch, slicing diagonally across the face. There was no time for tight turns, just one big hard drive as it picked up size and speed. Goog thought he knew about speed. He thought he understood size and power. But this was new. This was madness.

Goog could feel the brutal strength and see the massive wall of water in front of him. The wave was dredging heavy water up its face. He could drown out here and never be found. This coast was full of snags and underwater caves. If he wiped out here and the wave drove him down, he would be shoved into the reef and would never surface.

His board knew its job though and held its line beautifully.

It was performing exactly as it should, designed to handle size and power.

The lip of the wave began feathering and he shifted his weight forward for more speed. Ahead a tube was beginning to form, the wave pitching strongly. Fear welled up inside Goog. The wave was an elephant – fifteen foot from base to lip. This was decision time: if he proned-out, he would wind up on the point and cop a certain battering on the rocks; if he went for the tube, it could shut down and crush him.

He went for it. Pulling high on the wave near the turning lip and then dropping down, he rocketed into the barrel as it completed itself. Inside, the roar of water was deafening. The eye of the tube was beginning to close. Clouds rolled grey in the opening. There was a slow and terrible moment of fear, as he realised he wasn't going to make it. Then a burst of exhilaration as the wave spat him out, blowing a cloud of white water at his back. Goog carved a big turn, his inner rail buried deep, and then he slipped over the shoulder and surfed down the back of the wave to the whooping of the Beards and his mates.

For all the exhilaration he felt, Goog was glad it was over. Now he could sit out the rest of the session on the shoulder. No one would call him a coward after that wave.

The Beards donated one to Castro. It was a couple of feet smaller than Goog's but perfect in shape. He dropped down the face, slipped onto his board and made the bottom turn in one fluid motion. Castro had such a loose and comfortable style. He looked as if he was back home at *Boobs* or *Winki* on a four-foot day.

When Goog got back into the line-up, one of the Beards grinned at him. 'Nice one, buddy,' he said.

But Goog knew he had been terrified with the heaviness of all that water around him; that it was all bluff, an illusion spliced together from fear and necessity.

Back at the car, towelled dry and looking out at the sea, Goog felt lighter. He had been out there and survived. And, even better, everyone thought he had charged. He watched the seal-like blobs of the Beards, cruising to the shorebreak. They bodyboarded into the beach, coming up laughing after they were drilled into the hard sand. They tucked their big boards under their arms and walked slowly up the beach, turning every now and then as if they'd left something back out at sea. As they passed the car, one of them leant in through the window.

'Coming f'r a beer?'

Goog answered. 'Yeah, sure.'

The front bar was full of fishermen in tracky daks, sequined with fish scales and spattered with the odd dark string of blood. The wholesome smell of sour beer and fish struck them as they entered. Footy trophies cluttered a shelf above the bar and a stuffed eagle looked down from a wood-panelled wall. Aldo pointed up to it and grinned.

'What a beauty, eh,' he said to Castro, who ignored him and followed the Beards to the bar.

One of the Beards, Mal, ordered up seven pots and they went over and sat at a table. There were a couple of pokies in the corner and two of the Beards went off to run their wallets dry while Goog, Aldo and Castro sipped the froth off their beers and wondered how to start a conversation. It was usually easy for Castro but even he was struck dumb by these big men and the slow, confident way they moved around each other.

Mal broke into the silence. 'Going west, boys?'

Goog felt compelled to speak; he had been the hero out there at *Elephants*. 'Yeah, Margaret River.'

Mal and the other Beard looked at each other. 'Shit, Ron, we're in the presence of greatness.'

Aldo's brow folded over but he kept silent.

'Yeah, and then who knows? Maybe Indo. Eh, Castro?'

Castro nodded into his beer, not sure why Goog was suddenly in the driver's seat.

'And then maybe Sri Lanka,' continued Goog. 'Or hop on a charter boat and surf *Thunder Reef*.'

That caught Ron's attention. 'You guys wouldn't want to surf *Thunder*. Not since the resort bought the rights to it. Rights!' He slammed his beer on the table. 'It's fuckin ridiculous treating water like real estate.'

'Ron used to crew for a charter company, been all over the Pacific. Haven't you, Ron?'

'Yup.' Ron drained his glass and wiped the froth off his moustache. 'Anyone for another?'

While Ron was away at the bar, Mal said, 'Ron got into a bit of trouble out at *Thunder*, kept pretty quiet about it since he's been back. If you want to know about surf spots, though, he's your man. Knows the coast from here to W.A. and up east as far as the Reef.'

Ron came back with a tray of beers. Goog noticed his right thumb, split like a goat's foot, nail and all.

'Cheers,' said Castro. 'Mal was saying you're a bit of an expert on the breaks from here to W.A.'

'I reckon Mal says a bit more than he should sometimes.'

Ron shot Mal a dirty look but Mal was looking through to the lounge bar, where the Germans from the Twelve Apostles were trying to order beer. They spotted Aldo and headed back towards the door.

Castro asked, 'D'you know of a break in the Bight? Big-wave spot. These fishos we met called it *Ladders*.'

'Yeah, I reckon I know the spot,' said Ron. 'Pretty heavy, too. That's serious juice, boys, and big shark territory. Makes today look like a frolic by the seaside. Yeah, *Ladders*, surfed the spot with Larco. Remember Larry Mc— Mc—' He looked at Mal for help.

'Conners.'

'That's the man – Larry Conners. Craziest bastard you ever come across. Madder'n a cut snake. But could that fucker surf! Hooooh yeah.' Ron seemed to be warming to the topic. 'I watched it one day at about ten, maybe twelve foot. Thickest lip I ever seen in a wave. Push you to the bottom and hold you there. And holes all through the reef – lots of snag points. Reckon if more people knew about it, a lot more would drown. Course the biteys keep the reef nice and clean. Some big fuckin fish down there and no mistake. White Pointers – and I don't mean the bathin beauty type either. Anyway, where was I?'

'Ten, twelve foot, Ron,' Mal said.

Ron rubbed his nose with his forked thumb. 'Yeah, twelve foot and meaner than a ute load of pit-bulls. I mean gnarly with a capital N! You don't want to go out there under-gunned. You want to be fully committed – that wave can sense your fear like a dog. The fucker'll eat you alive.'

Goog took a deep swallow of beer and looked at Castro. His eyes were shining with madness – the same look he had at Johanna when the fishos were talking.

'D'you win?' Mal asked the poker-machine Beards as they came back via the bar.

'Nuh. Bloody rigged they are.'

'Let's grab a couple of slabs and head up to Tusker's, eh?' Mal had drained his second beer and was keen to get out of the pub. 'Come on, drink up. You guys comin?' He nodded at Goog, Aldo and Castro. 'You can crash at Tusker's if you want.'

Goog looked at Castro and they both nodded *yes*.

Aldo, who had been silent for most of the day, said, 'I need some sleep. You bastards kept me up all night.' He felt himself being edged out by the Beards; he was losing his position of power. 'And you can't get there or back without a car.'

The Beards found this pretty funny. Mal said, 'Leave him here, the miserable prick. We'll drop youse two back in town in the morning.'

Goog grinned at Castro. Of course they had to accept. It wasn't every day a surfing community took you in and made you welcome. Aldo would get over it.

The track to Tusker's was steep and rutted. They were crammed in the back of Ron's van – Goog, Castro, Tusker, the other Beard (Simmo), six boards and a couple of bags of old pipis. Ron and Mal were up front and had Thin Lizzie cranked up on the stereo. Castro was in heaven.

Tusker's place turned out to be a six-metre-square aluminium shed with a pot-belly at one end and a double bed at the other. Candles and Tilley lamps threw out a yellow glow. The floor was made from old packing crates and thin yellow weeds were struggling up the walls. The air was heavy with kerosene fumes.

Simmo stuffed a pile of kindling and some newspaper in the pot-belly and slopped in a cupful of kero. When he put a match to it, it sputtered for a while before the flame took hold. The burning kindling sent a roar up the chimney and they all moved closer to the warmth.

'Here's to civilisation!' said Ron as they cracked open their stubbies. After a long and thoughtful drink, Ron spoke again. 'Tusker's got some charts around here somewhere. Where are them charts, Tusker?'

Tusker pointed Ron to a battered cardboard box beside the old kero fridge.

Ron grabbed the charts and spread them out on the bed. Goog and Castro looked over his shoulder at the coastline of the Bight. The thin line of the highway crossed the page from edge to edge.

'Here. You drive off here.' Ron put his split thumb on the map. 'There's a bizarre-looking rock at the start of the track – looks like it's been burnt black. It's not like any other rock out there. You drive down the track maybe four or five k's.' Ron snaked his thumb to the sea. 'And then you come to a big open spot.' He poked his finger down near the water. 'I mean, it's all pretty open out there, but this spot's been swept clear of stones and there's campfires all over it. Just park up there and walk to the edge of the cliffs. It'll blow your mind.' He raised his eyes to Goog and Castro, who nodded and fought off too-big smiles.

'If it's going off, I reckon it's one of the best waves in the world. Further out it could hold up to about forty foot. Nice big slab of sloping reef just dipping itself into the Southern Ocean.' Ron's eyes were yellow with candlelight. 'Remember two things, though – big water and mean fish. Don't under-estimate this break.'

Goog stared at the chart, at the big sweep of the Bight, the contours dropping steeply away from the continent. He looked at Castro, who had begun to sweat, even though the fire had hardly bitten the edge off the chill.

'I hate to break up this little sewing circle but there's some beer to be drunk.' Mal swung a sixpack onto the bed. 'You guys are crazy if you go there. This man,' he pointed at Ron, 'is off his head. Don't even listen to him.'

Goog wondered if this wasn't good advice. But Castro was running his finger over the map, from the highway to the sea.

The next morning drizzled into view through Tusker's plastic-sheet windows. The duct tape that held them onto the wall was peeling and water was running down to the floor. At least the weeds were getting watered. Goog woke up next to four bearded, snoring men. Castro was asleep in a board bag, tufts of his hair poking from the top.

Goog's head was pulsing with his heartbeat and his tongue was stuck to the roof of his mouth. He needed water. Outside, he stared at the sky while he took a leak. He stood in the rain for five minutes, until he worked out he was getting wet. He opened his mouth and tried catching some drops on his tongue but it just wasn't enough so he trudged back inside.

The fridge was full of nothing. No juice or water. There was a solitary beer lurking at the back but Goog knew he just couldn't. He shook Castro awake and together they raised Ron and got him to drive them back to town.

Aldo was alone in the caravan park, frying up eggs and bacon on the barbecue. There was a pile of twenty-cent pieces piled near the egg carton. He was sulking.

'G'day, Aldo,' Castro managed through the thick fog of his hangover.

'You guys are fucken hopeless. Look at ya. What a pair of dickwits.' Aldo was acting like their mother, but with considerably worse language. He was biting his thumbnail, making it bleed.

'What's for breakfast?' Goog asked. He was just making conversation. There was no way he could stomach eggs and bacon.

'This isn't for you. Go and get your own fucken breakfast. You guys are fair dinkum parasites.'

'Lighten up, Aldo,' said Castro as he walked off towards the shower block.

Goog wandered over to the shops and bought a chocolate milk. When he got back, Aldo was sitting in the Kingswood with the engine running. Castro was flat out over the bonnet, drawing heat from the engine.

Aldo spat out the window. 'You comin, or what? Or are you going to hang out with your new mates now? Soon as you find someone else with a car, you piss off and leave me. Good mates you are.'

Goog and Castro got in and Aldo ripped up the grass with his rear tyres. They flew past the office, fishtailing and spraying gravel. The manager clambered out the door and wrote their rego down on the back of his hand. But they were gone and never coming back.

6

THIRD HOUSE ON THE RIGHT

It was obviously important to some urban planner that every major Australian city look identical, so Adelaide scored a freeway too. Now every interstate visitor could feel at home as they flew in on the fast, flat bitumen. The Kingswood droned along at one-ten, slapping the cat's eyes as Aldo wandered between lanes. The dash rattled, gum leaves worked their way through the vents and whipped into Castro who was sleeping with his toes smearing up the windscreen. Eventually he stretched and groaned and pulled the cap back from his eyes.

'We there yet?'

'Soon, mate. Soon.' Aldo seemed almost excited. It was the cheeriest Goog had seen him since he dobbed Jasper in to the police back in Lorne.

'So who are these friends of yours we're staying with?' Goog wondered who could possibly be mates with Aldo. He only did it from necessity. God knows what Castro saw in him.

'Just friends. Brothers, actually.'

Goog said, 'You don't have any brothers, Aldo.'

'Not that kind of brothers, dickbrain. More like brothers-in-arms.'

'You mean you're part of a Dire Straits fan club,' said Castro, champion of retro-humour.

'The Brotherhood of Aryan Responsi-Bility,' Aldo broke the last word in two, to allow the capital letters to do their work. 'BARB is a national organisation that promotes pride in racial purity and harmony through uniformity.'

Goog shot a questioning look at Castro. *What the f—?*

'Have you known these guys long?' asked Castro.

'I've never met them. But the Brotherhood is my true family.'

Aldo stared calmly ahead, through the clouds, grey and life-less as old pot scourers, and into a more perfect world. The closer they got to Adelaide, the more together he seemed, as if he was drawing strength from the city where his *true family* existed. Goog didn't like this change in behaviour. Aldo the Aryan Brother scared the crap out of him. What was all this *true family, racial purity* shit? That wasn't Aldo; the sentence hadn't contained *fuck*, in any of its forms. Castro rummaged in the glovebox for answers and Goog pretended to sleep. It wouldn't be too long before they got to the bottom of things.

The directions were written on the back of a beer mat that Aldo refused to let either Goog or Castro see. He drew air in through his nose and explained patiently, 'Youse dickheads'll just lose us.'

The beer mat had been involved in a bit of action since receiving the directions – corners had been ripped off for roach material and its surface was flaked like a leper's back. They skittled through the Adelaide traffic, Aldo's hand jumping mechanically between horn and gears. He held the mat between his smoking fingers and flipped it up every now and then to glance at it. Goog caught a glimpse of some kind of map, a blue soup of lines and names. Surely it was impossible to map out an entire city on something so small.

The houses all looked the same to Goog, row on row of them parked up against the street. The shops looked oddly familiar, too, and so did the scruffy park with its bent-waterpipe play equipment. Nearby a group of workmen were pulling up the concrete, three of them leaning wearily on shovels while a fourth jackhammered the pavement. One of the leaners was wearing a Chicago Bulls hat. Heavy with fat, he was sweating like an ox, even though it was seventeen degrees outside. He looked up at them as they drove by and Goog thought he saw a faint glimmer of recognition wander over the man's face.

Then Goog twigged. It all looked the same, because this was the second time they were seeing it. Aldo had been pulling big deja-vu loops around the city. This was the same set of lights they had been caught at before. The same boy on the park bench was still forcing his fist into his mouth. And that had to be the same goat statue, there was no forgetting it.

'Hey, Aldo, you lost?' asked Goog.

'No, dickwad, I know exactly where I'm going. What makes you a fucken expert all of a sudden? I gotta compass inside my head that always points me in the right direction.'

Yeah, well, that compass is as faulty as the rest of your equip-ment, thought Goog. But out loud, 'I think we've been here before. That statue there,' he pointed to the burnt-orange goat, horns-up in a patch of grass, 'I've seen that ugly thing before.'

'What're you saying, dickcheese? That I don't know where I'm going? Coz I do.'

It took another hour before Aldo pulled over to a phone box.

They were almost out of petrol. He didn't say a word, didn't even look at Goog and Castro, as he went to make the call. He was silent when he got back in, but he had the cover from the *White Pages (A-K)* with him and its margins were infested with his wonky handwriting.

They seemed to get there quickly after that. No more than ten minutes and they were sitting in front of a red-brick house – a small, mean place with cracks spreading between its joints. It was two houses from the main road and, as the trucks rumbled by, the few unbroken windows rattled in their frames. Aldo seemed happy and nervous as he led them up the garden path, another side of him Goog had never seen. He smoothed his scalp with his palm and bounced as he walked. He talked way more than usual.

'Now, you guys, behave, okay. These are my friends and I want you to show some fucken respect, okay. You got that? Got it?' But he was smiling as he said it. 'Now just be natural. Act yourself, okay. I don't want no fucken problems. No hassles, okay. This is important.'

Okay. Okay. Okay.

The grass on either side of the path was so long that it formed a corridor. Silver snail tracks wound over the concrete. The front door had a notice pinned to it:

This building is illegally occupied. The occupants have fourteen days from the time of this notice to vacate the premises.

Goog glanced at his watch and noticed that time was up yesterday. The door showed signs of violence – several marks that could have been made with a crowbar. The frosted glass was missing two of three panels and plywood had been u-nailed over the openings. There was a padbolt screwed at an unprofessional angle below the handle and the words *Come And Get Us!* were scratched into the paintwork below the eviction notice.

Aldo knocked. Before long there was the sound of bolts being drawn and a bunch of tattooed knuckles appeared round the door. The hand was replaced by a shaved head and sullen grey eyes. The head had a swastika tattooed like a third eye in the middle of the brow. The head's nostrils were crusted with white powder. On the wall behind the head was a print of dogs playing pool: a bulldog smoking a cigar, a ridgeback chalking up his cue. There wasn't a poodle in sight.

Things were freeze-framed like that for a moment – the silent head, the still safety-chained door and them on the outside, waiting for something to happen.

'Brother Peter?' Aldo smiled his big-dog smile, ear to ear and dripping slobber.

'He's not here.' The skinhead was nervous. He went to close the door but Aldo's hand stopped it.

'He knows we were coming, I called him before. Look, here, I got this. Proof.' He showed the guy a card with a small red logo in the corner, the name Peter Maelstrom and a mobile number. 'I'm Brother Alan from Torquay and this is bro— this is Goog and Castro. They're, ah . . . friends.'

The skinhead looked at them for a moment, grinding his teeth hard enough for all to hear, and said, 'You'd better come in then. You,' he pointed a shaky finger at Goog, 'better leave that camera in the car.'

What sort of a nuthouse is this? thought Goog as he buried his camera under the sleeping bag in the rear of the wagon. Everyone he seemed to meet these days was camera shy. First the hitcher, Jasper, and now these freaky Brothers. Goog felt his arms and legs buzz with a familiar sensation. *Fight or flight*, they had called it in biology; he hoped he would need neither.

The house was not much better inside than out. It smelt sharply of piss and damp blooms of mould were climbing the walls. The letters *SS* had been carved into the plaster near the pool-playing dogs. Coffee cups festered on the damp carpet. Someone had tried to hack a doorway in one wall. It led nowhere, but exposed the stud frame like a ribcage and oozed fat clots of dust onto the skirting boards.

'Peter's out on business. He won't be home until this evening.' The skinhead spoke with a soft, almost English accent, his shoulders jerking involuntarily. 'Wait if you want to, I have some things to do.' He walked across the hall and opened a door that had been painted with a pair of crossed swords. Goog caught a glimpse of something that looked like scales inside the room and a scattering of ziplock bags on a table before the skinhead shut the door behind him.

Castro rubbed his hands together. 'May's well make a cuppa.' The kitchen had to be nearby. The smell of rancid fat coming from behind a door let him know he was getting close. Goog moved up behind him and stifled a gag. It was the kitchen, all right. Or what was left of one.

Dirty plates rose high above the benchtops, pizza boxes gaped like rabbit traps between gatherings of apple cores and toast crusts. Castro grabbed the electric jug that was hooked over the door handle and, nudging it into the full sink, turned on the tap. There was a burping sound but no water. It looked as if the water had been disconnected, but not before it had started a plague of wet rot beneath the cabinet. The toe of Castro's runner broke open the spongy boards as he walked away.

It took some effort to reach the fridge, and by the time Goog and Castro had crunched and squished their way over there, they weren't that curious to see inside. Unfortunately the door was open and Goog couldn't help but notice an inch or so of green fluid bubbling in the vegie crisper. He felt his stomach rise again. The fridge was empty, apart from an onion on the top shelf. The onion had grown a bright green sprout that had turned back on itself and was beginning to exit the fridge. It was the only symbol of hope in the whole room.

Aldo had finished admiring the artwork in the hall and squelched his way into the room. 'Fuck me!' he said.

The words caught the attention of a big brown rat that was feasting on chop fat in the open griller. It eyed them with distrust, its sharp little teeth flecked with pieces of tin foil. Obviously it would not give up its hard-won meal without a struggle. Castro bent down slowly and grabbed a claw hammer from the floor. The rat followed his moves, its whiskers twitching and the muscles in its haunches rippling like water. Castro worked his way slowly towards it, moving sideways to present as small an area as possible to the rat. He drew the hammer up slowly.

Too slowly.

The rat flew at him. Castro smashed the hammer onto the griller, sending fat into the air like snow. The rat landed claws-out on Castro's jumper and scrabbled its way rapidly up to his neck. He yelped, dropped the hammer and began raking at it with his hands. As he struggled to grab the rat, it worked its way around his jumper and onto his back.

Goog was dumbstruck. He couldn't move, couldn't decide if the scene was *pure comedy* or *mild danger*. He knew rats carried disease and were dangerous if cornered, especially with claw hammers. They left sinking ships and had starring roles in horror movies. His hand went to his neck and felt for his camera strap, but it was in the car. Should he help Castro, photograph him, or laugh?

Castro fell on the floor and began to roll over and over, trying to squash the rat into submission. By his third roll, he was sticky with chop fat, and chicken bones had started to glue themselves to his legs. The rat was still firmly attached to his jumper.

Then Aldo stepped up. Swinging his boot at the rat, he kicked it across the room and onto the opposite wall. It hit the flaking plaster with a slap and fell to the floor.

Castro pulled himself up onto his elbows. He looked at the rat. Its head was bent back at a strange angle and a thread of blood ran from its mouth.

For once in his life, Aldo was a hero.

'How's I supposed to know it was your fucken rat?'

They were gathered around the rat on the kitchen floor: Goog, Aldo, Castro and the owner of the *fucken rat*.

Brother Peter had been given the rat when he had moved out of home. It was a present from his mother. The rat was called Mr Magic and was four years old. It was most definitely dead.

Aldo's hero status was dropping fast.

Brother Peter was tall and so fair Goog could almost see through him. His skin was stretched tight over his cheekbones and he had no eyelashes or eyebrows. His head was shaved bald and, under forty watts of kitchen light, he looked like a snake.

'Grief is an overrated emotion,' said Brother Peter, 'Love and grief. Extremely overrated.' He put his fist to his mouth.

'I mean, what kind of pet is a fucken rat, anyway? Now a

dog, that's different. I wouldn't have killed a dog,' Aldo said, with all the sensitivity of a stormtrooper, but he was beginning to cry. 'I would never have killed a dog.'

'It's okay, mate,' Castro whispered. 'You didn't know.'

Brother Peter picked up a milk carton from the kitchen bench and poured the lumpy contents into the sink. He pulled the top apart so it became an open box – a casket.

'Hate and fear. Now those are emotions.' Brother Peter got hold of Mr Magic's tail and dropped him into the carton. He carried him out of the kitchen door and into the backyard. Aldo, Castro and Goog stood quietly, looking at each other.

'I didn't fucken mean it!' blubbered Aldo. 'It was going to kill you, Castro. I had to do something.'

Out in the yard, Brother Peter was chopping at the soil with an axe, trying to make a deep enough hole for Mr Magic. Aldo, Castro and Goog stepped through the knee-high grass towards him. Castro took a seat on a derelict clothes drier; Goog and Aldo stood on either side of him.

Brother Peter looked up at them, his face dusty and emotionless. He grabbed Mr Magic's milk carton coffin and placed it carefully in the hole he had made. With his foot, he scraped soil over the carton and went back inside. Aldo flattened a Pepsi can under the heel of his boot and poked it in the ground like a headstone.

When they traipsed back inside, Brother Peter was leaning over the sink, looking blankly out the window.

'Brother Aldo,' he said, 'I need to show you something. Follow me.'

Aldo looked at Castro and Goog for support. He had just killed a man's rat and now that man wanted him to follow him somewhere. Alone!

Brother Peter stopped at the kitchen door. 'You can bring your little friends with you.'

Castro grimaced at Goog, but they followed Aldo, who was glowing with pride and duty, into the hallway. Brother Peter stopped in front of the door with the crossed swords and knocked. After a while there was the sound of a bolt being drawn and the skinhead appeared.

'I need the key,' said Brother Peter, leaning on the door frame.

The man shut the door and the boys could hear him clomping across the bare floorboards of the room. There was a rasp, and another, as a drawer was opened and shut, and then the man clomped back over to the door. His hand appeared with the key and Brother Peter took it without a word.

The door in the adjacent wall was painted red and had a sturdy padlock. Brother Peter unlocked it and they followed him inside. The room was lit with a blue strip light, so it took a while before their eyes adjusted. Eventually they could see a large desk along the far wall and a window blocked out with plywood. The desk was bristling with high-tech gadgets – a laser printer, a scanner, a CD burner. Goog knew enough about computers to realise this gear was worth a few dollars.

Brother Peter turned the computer on. His face glowed death-white from the screen's radiation. 'I want you to have a look at this, Brother Aldo. I think you'll be impressed.'

Aldo was relieved to have been forgiven, to be back on good terms with the Brotherhood. 'You fucken bet I will!'

There was a groan from behind them and Goog turned to see a man rising from a bed in the far corner of the room. He was wearing a Ren and Stimpy shirt and wrap-around sunglasses.

Brother Peter walked over to him. 'Brother Torquil, I trust you slept well?'

'Slept like shit and you know it. Have you brought me some candy?' said Torquil.

'No candy, not until you've *sung for your supper*. Where's the box?'

Torquil reached under the bed and pulled out a green cashbox.

'And the key?' said Brother Peter.

Torquil pulled at a leather thong around his neck and produced a key. He unlocked the box and handed it to Brother Peter.

'Good. I just want to show Brother Aldo and his little friends your handiwork. Torquil is quite the genius, aren't you, Torquil?'

Torquil smiled blackly at the three of them. He looked bad. His eyes were sunken and there were scabs over his face and on the backs of his hands.

Brother Peter walked back over to the desk and put the cashbox on it. Flipping the lid open, he pulled out a fat plastic disk and quickly shut the lid again.

'This is a Zip disk. Holds about two-fifty meg of information. That's nearly two hundred times what a floppy can hold, so a Zip is more like a small hard drive. Only it's removable, so wherever I go, the disk goes too. You following this, Brother Aldo?'

'Ah . . . yeah. Yup, no worries. Two-fifty megs.' Aldo nodded like his head was loose.

Brother Peter put the thick, red disk into a drive and clicked on an icon on the computer screen. A website home-page opened with a sepia image of Adolf Hitler addressing the crowd. In huge red script were the words *Brotherhood of Aryan ResponsiBility,* and underneath them *watchdog of the pure world*. Brother Peter clicked on a spinning swastika. The next page came up.

> *The Brotherhood of Aryan ResponsiBility is an organisation that campaigns for the rights of White citizens the world over . . .*

Brother Peter clicked again. And again. Page after page of information and photos glorifying the Nazi cause.

> *Reports of the Holocaust have been much exaggerated. Pro-Semitic forces within government have seen fit . . .*

Photos of smiling blond-haired children, of old propaganda posters, ugly cartoons.

> *Immigration is the enemy of a pure race. It has been estimated that 98 per cent of the world's surface will be polluted by mixed blood . . .*

Goog felt ill, his mouth dried up and his limbs began to ache – the old *fight or flight* kicking in again. What the hell was Aldo mixed up in, and why were they being dragged into it?

'This is grouse. This is just fucken ace,' said Aldo.

A page of links came up – hate sites, Nazi collectibles, image banks. Goog looked at Castro but he wasn't even paying attention. He had opened the lid to the cashbox and drawn out a fifty-dollar note. He flipped it up between his fingers so Goog could see it. Goog shook his head. *No way, Castro,* he mouthed. Castro pulled him over to the far side of the room.

'Listen, Goog,' he whispered, 'there's over three grand in there. Three grand! We could go to Indo right now, just take the box and run.'

Goog looked at Torquil lying on the bed, holding his stomach. 'Shhh, what about him?' he said, pointing his thumb at the groaning body.

'He hardly knows we're here. Goog, this is a full-on opportunity. Plus we'd be doing the world a service. Imagine what these scumbags could do with three thousand bucks.'

'No way, Castro. No way!' Goog walked back over to the computer on jelly legs. What was Castro thinking, these maniacs could kill them. On screen, Hitler and his adoring fans were back.

Brother Peter said, 'So, Brother Aldo, are you committed to the cause? Do you have what it takes to be a soldier in this holy war?'

'Look, yeah, I do. I do. My Uncle Dougie says I got real promise. He's a member of the Melbourne Chapter. You probably know him.'

'I don't know any *Uncle Dougies*. But I do know the first step on the road to winning this war is dissemination of information.'

'Dis . . . wha?' Aldo looked confused.

'That's what this website is about. When Torquil gets it up and running next month, the whole world will know about us. Of course, it's important not to allow this information to get into the wrong hands. Some people like to suppress the truth.'

Brother Peter popped the Zip disk out of the drive and held it up.

'That is why we have only one copy of the site, right here on this disk. This small piece of plastic holds the fate of the entire White race. It is totally portable and easy to conceal. It is also very hard to find.' He pulled the cashbox across the desk, away from the lustful eyes of Castro. 'Now, to your part in the whole thing, Brother Aldo. We have some leaflets we'd like you to deliver. You're taking a trip and that is the perfect opportunity for reaching out to the wider community. Remember that to turn vacation into vocation, you only have to change one letter.'

'O,' said Aldo.

'Pardon?' said Brother Peter.

'O. That's the letter you have to change. You swap it with A and you get *vocation*. I did spellin at school. I was pretty fucken good at it too.'

'I'm sure you were, Brother Aldo.'

There was some frantic knocking at the door and Brother Peter went over and opened it.

It was the skinhead with the third-eye tattoo. He was raking at his cheek with his fingers, his hand was shaking badly. 'There's pigs out the front,' he said between clenched teeth. 'Cops! Two cars and a dog van. What do we do?'

'Get rid of the stuff. And for Christ's sake, calm down,' said Brother Peter. 'I'll take care of things here.'

He slammed the door and grabbed a cardboard box from the corner, handing it to Aldo. 'Here are the leaflets. Take them and go!'

The boys started for the door but Brother Peter stopped them. 'Not that way. Out the window and over the back fence.'

There was a loud knocking at the front door. Louder. The sound of splintering wood and throaty growls.

Goog saw Brother Peter move towards the cashbox but, before he got to it, Torquil dropped from the bed and grabbed his ankle. 'What's going on? You said I'd get my candy,' he said as Peter dropped to the floor. Castro moved from the far side of the room and over Peter's body. Shoving Goog through the window, he followed. Something inside his jumper clunked as he cleared the frame.

They caught up with Aldo and ran down the side of the house. As Aldo vaulted the back fence, his box split open and pamphlets spilled from it. He grabbed handfuls and stuffed them back into the broken carton, holding it against his chest as they ran towards the main road.

Castro was carrying something. Something bulky underneath his jumper that was making it hard for him to run. They split up at a row of shops, Aldo and Goog running to the left, Castro taking a small street to the right.

The sound of sirens filled the air. Aldo was tiring; the box was too heavy to carry.

'Ditch the box, Aldo!'

'No fucken way.' Aldo's chest was heaving with the effort.

They kept running up the street. When they got to the end, they saw Castro coming towards them. The lump beneath his jumper was gone. Goog was as curious as a death-row cat. 'Where's your lump?' he panted at Castro.

Castro looked at him as if he was mad. 'My what?'

'The thing under your jumper.'

'That was nothing,' Castro replied, smoothing the belly of his jumper flat.

'But —' Goog started in.

Castro's eyes were full of fire, his head slightly to one side. 'It was nothing, Goog,' he said slowly.

Aldo sat on the pavement still holding the box of precious pamphlets. He was hugging it to his chest and rocking slightly.

Goog bent down, his hands on his knees, swallowing away the sickness that was welling up inside. 'That was close,' he said. 'That was way too close. Imagine if we'd got caught up in all that shit. Great start to the trip. Thanks a lot, Aldo!'

Aldo looked up from his box. 'It's not my fault. You can't blame me.'

Castro said, 'Shut up, you guys, okay. I'm trying to think.' He paused for a while, tugged at his little goatee and then continued. 'We'll wait here for a while. Lie low. And then sneak back and get the car. They're not after us. There's nothing to connect us with those psychos.'

'They're not —' Aldo began, but Castro silenced him with a raised hand.

When they rounded the corner half an hour later, there was only one cop car parked in front of the house. Retreating, they grouped around an old postbox.

Castro pinched the bridge of his nose and closed his eyes. 'Okay, here's what we do. We stroll up to the car, nice and easy, like we're the most innocent dudes on the planet. Don't even look at the cop car, just get into the Kingswood, start up and drive off, nice and slow. You got it?' He opened his eyes and stared hard at Goog and Aldo until they nodded.

While they walked down the street towards the car, Goog rubbed the sweat from his palms and looked at his goal – the gleaming, pile-of-shit Kingswood at the far end of the street. Aldo was still carrying his stupid big box.

They passed the cop car. One cop was asleep, a circle of drool on one shoulder. The other was deep into the *Advertiser*'s sports section and was totally unaware they were passing. Aldo dropped his box in the rear of the Kingswood and let Goog and Castro in. They put on their seatbelts like law-abiding citizens and Aldo started the car.

Or tried to.

He tried again. Click. Click. The battery was dead.

'Whadda we fucken do now, Mr Fucken Plan-man?' Aldo asked Castro.

'I'll sort it. Don't worry,' said Castro. He got out of the Kingswood and walked over to the police car.

He stood at the driver's side window and had a conversation that involved a lot of hand gestures. When the conversation ended, he strutted back to the Kingswood.

'Just call me Mr Fixit,' he said as the cop car hung a noisy U-turn in the street and ended up nose-to-nose with Aldo's car.

'Pop the bonnet,' said the cop.

Aldo did as he was told and the other cop came out from the boot of the cop car with a set of jumper leads. They connected the two batteries and Aldo fired the Kingswood into life.

One of the cops bent over the engine for a while. He beckoned Aldo out of the car with his oil-covered finger.

'See this,' he said, pointing inside the engine bay, 'That's your earth lead and it belongs on here.' He pushed it to the engine block where it used to be bolted. 'Get it fixed today, all right.'

Aldo nodded.

'And one more thing.'

Aldo hesitated on his way back to the driver's seat.

The cop slammed the bonnet shut. 'This heap of shit needs a tune, bad.' He went back to his car and reversed down the street.

Aldo got in the Kingswood. 'Shit, Castro, what did you fucken say to them?'

Castro grinned. 'My dad does the Adelaide run twice a month. Knows a lot of cops. He gave me a name in case I got in trouble.'

'Well, why did we run in the first place?' asked Goog.

'It was only a name, not a magic spell. They'd have to take us in for questioning if they caught us in the house.' Castro looked Aldo square in the eye. 'Your dear Brother Peter dobbed us in. Said three young guys had been hanging around. Took quite a bit of explaining until they believed we were nothing to do with the Brotherhood.'

'But Brother Peter, there's no way —'

'There's no bloody loyalty there, Aldo. Forget about them, they're scumbags. Let's get going, before the cops change their minds.'

It was getting dark as they left Adelaide behind. Once clear of the city, they pulled over in a truck stop and slept in the car till dawn. Then, with the sky bursting yellow at the horizon, they started towards the Nullarbor. The day was bright – clean and crisp as a new season apple. Castro drove. There was no way Aldo could argue: Castro had saved them from a whole load of heaviness.

Goog looked out over the paddocks, the endless lines of fencing wire and bent star pickets. He closed his eyes and tried to picture the ocean, its soft emulsion and wheeling birds, the power it had to cure.

Drowning in inland boredom, he bent into the back to get his camera. Nestled among their gear was Aldo's battered cardboard box, the one that Peter had given to him. There was a pile of pamphlets stuffed inside. Glossy paper, a rectangular sheet folded twice; money no object for the Brotherhood. He pulled one out and read *Seven Ways To A Cleaner Brighter Future*.

Below the heading was a photo of a young boy of around six or seven. Goog flipped over the pamphlet to look for a photo credit. Instead he found *Cover photo of Peter Maelstrom (1975)*. He went back to the cover. It *was* Brother Peter. Even as a child he looked like a snake. Goog opened up the pamphlet.

> *The Brotherhood of Aryan ResponsiBility was founded in 1988 as a reaction to the gross inequality experienced by people of Aryan descent everywhere. History has taught us that the racial inferiority of Asians, Blacks and Jews has done little to economically disadvantage them. This inequality has been addressed at times . . .*

A lump of bile rolled in Goog's stomach. He looked at the back of Aldo's fat neck, where a dribble of sweat was beginning to run through the emerging black hairs. They were a sick bunch of bastards, these Brothers.

He smoothed the pamphlet out flat and turned it longways on his knee. He brought the bottom edge of the sheet to meet the right-hand side, folding down a triangle. He tore off the rectangular dag of paper at the top edge of the sheet and then unfolded the triangle. That left him with a square of paper – the starting point for an origami crane.

Goog remembered last summer, sitting on Marcella's verandah folding cranes, Marcella's quick fingers pushing in the creases, birds evolving before their eyes until the deck was covered in them. It was hot and the smell of wattle blossom floated in from the yard, thick and dusty. He remembered wishing the day would last forever, that everything would remain as simple and perfect as the photos he took. They'd gathered armfuls of paper cranes and strung them on satay sticks. The mobile was still hanging in Joshua's room. He would be six months old now, fat and happy like a TV baby. Marcella's sister used to hand him to Goog when his head was still too loose on his neck. It scared the shit out of Goog. That and the look Marcella gave him when Josh was in his arms.

The first crane was difficult. He could hardly remember the folds and didn't have a hard, flat surface to work on. But by the sixth one the paper birds were neater, the creases sharp and clean. Aldo was fast asleep with his head bent over the back of the seat. He would wake up with a killer pain in his neck. His mouth was open and he was gagging on the dry air. Goog folded crane number forty. They were piled up inside the car like a snowdrift, on the floor and over the remaining seat. Castro didn't seem to notice. He hadn't used the rear-view mirror in the last hour.

At eighty-five birds, the box was empty, apart from the printer's reorder form. Goog folded that up as well and, rolling the window down a quarter of the way, released the first bird. It tore out of his hand and shot from the car at a hundred clicks. The next one he threw upward and watched through the rear window as it nested in the grille of a cattle truck. He tossed a handful of ten out the window and saw them flock and scatter over the highway. They batted up against the windows of oncoming cars and lodged in stock fences. The last one was caught by a stationary cyclist. Goog saw him unfold the paper as their car flew away from him.

Ten kilometres down the road, Goog realised what he had done.

They were heading in the direction of Ceduna, skirting around the Eyre Peninsula, even though Goog was sure he could smell salt in the wind. Castro laughed at him, saying it was probably salinity dredged up from the soil, and flew past the left fork that would take them to the sea. He was on a mission now, all he wanted was to surf the desert break the fishos and the Beards had talked about. He didn't even want to discuss Margaret River or any of the opportunities in between. Nothing else seemed to matter. The trip had switched from being a surfari into being just one long drive to a break. Goog and Aldo were being swept along with it.

A few hundred kilometres north were the salt lakes and the holes where men had grubbed for opals. Goog could see the white blotches on the map and the cool blue of the ocean curving into the Bight. Iron Knob, Kimba, Kyancutta, Minnipa – the place names were as hard to swallow as the dry air drumming in through the windows. At Ceduna they would start to cross *the Paddock*, the great blanket of desert also known as the Nullarbor. Goog had thought it was an Aboriginal word but the blurry tourist brochure they picked up in Port Augusta said *null arbor* was Latin for *without trees*.

This was definitely no place for Latin.

They stopped for fuel in somewhere so small it was lucky to have a pub. While Aldo burped fuel into the tank, Goog and Castro went inside for a beer.

The door was open and it was hotter inside than out. Sand dusted the floorboards like icing sugar. There was a single weary-looking customer at the bar.

'Beer, thanks.'

'Two?'

'Yup.' Castro spooned some coins onto the chipped bar. The publican belched a heady mix of garlic and rum over the counter and poured the beers. Dumping the dirty glasses in front of Goog and Castro, he retreated into the shadows with a water-damaged copy of *People* magazine and carried on chewing his fatty Polish sausage.

Someone with a bit of time on their hands had carved a likeness of Jesus on the bar's black enamelled surface. A terry-towelling runner advertising Emu Ale swaddled the Son of God's head like a turban. The walls were covered in postcards and old money. One- and two-dollar notes nested beside drachmas and deutschmarks. The postcards were from Tokyo and Reykjavik and Majorca and Birmingham. There was even one that said *Greetings from Torquay*.

The guy at the other end of the bar looked like an untidy crow. He eyed them up unsteadily and then said, 'Where you fellas off to?'

'W.A., mate.' Castro kept his eyes on the wall.

'Yeah?' said the Crow, raising his eyebrows at the unlikely suggestion. 'Whatcha wanna go there for?'

'Surf.' Castro didn't want to talk to the Crow; he had nothing to offer them but beer burps and bullshit. Goog framed him up with his camera as he tripped his way towards them. 'Youse guys surfers?' he asked.

'Yup,' said Castro into his beer glass.

Goog clicked the shutter. The Crow cracked open his beak,

smiled and said, 'Not much surf round here, eh.'

Castro looked back out the grimy window to the street. 'Yeah, we'd noticed.'

'Down the Bight, though, mate. Big? Shit, waves like bloody mountains down there!'

Goog's pulse quickened. Castro was paying attention now.

'You been down there?' he asked.

'Yup. Used to be a helicopter pilot. Used to take touros out on joy flights and stuff like that.'

Bullshit. Goog doubted if the man could pilot a skateboard at the moment but he seemed a likeable enough guy, just a small-town waster. Something about him reminded Goog of Mad Alice. What had she said when they last met?

The man continued. 'Used to go out and spot whales and that. Whales and sharks. Big sharks, mate. Like bloody tanks they were. Like bloody road trains.'

Castro sipped his beer, his eye squarely on the Crow. 'And the surf?'

'Big, too. Twenty foot, easy, mate. S'huge. You'll need to swallow your fear to surf there, boys.' He winked a bleary-eyed wink at Goog.

Those were the words that Alice had used. Those or some like them. Or had he just imagined it? Something about swallowing fear. Goog took a swallow of beer instead and framed the Crow again. Click, just as he was opening his mouth to speak, yellow teeth, black gums.

'Had to do a rescue down there, once,' the Crow continued. 'Some waxhead got mauled by a shark. We had to chopper him to Adelaide. The bastard nearly carked it.' He paused, grabbed a handful of beer nuts and stuffed them in his mouth. 'I useta be a truckie. Drove all over this country till I found this place.

I seen it all and this is definertly the best spot. Definertly.' He nodded once to prove it and fell forward off his chair.

Goog eyed the postcard wall, the cigarette trough full of fag ends and lung oysters. He stared out into the flaring white day and the dust blowing up the highway. *Definertly the best spot.* Goog doubted it. To top it off, Aldo appeared in the doorway.

'You poofs ready to roll?'

They downed the rest of their beers and left. The drunk waved to them from the door.

'Be careful of them sharks, mate. They're big,' he called after them. As they walked out of the shade thrown by the pub, they could still hear him, 'Big! Fuckin big! Big as trucks, mate! Big as road trains!'

'I'm drivin,' said Aldo as they neared the car. Castro threw him the keys. It was hard to tell if Castro had lost ground or was just tired of being at the wheel. Aldo cranked up the old Beast and swung her onto the highway. Goog popped off a couple of shots of the pub as Aldo stomped on the accelerator. Click, click, the Crow in the doorway, the spinning meat-pie sign, the sagging iron roof and wedge-tail eagles spiralling through the big blue sky.

Then it was back to the straight edges of blacktop and the rotting piles of roadkill.

At Ceduna they still had half a tank and Aldo did not want to stop, even though they were low on water. Even though they were heading into the desert.

CROSSING THE
PADDOCK

7

PANTYHOSE MAN

Goog was reading over Castro's shoulder, a battered op-shop book with over half the front cover missing. What was left looked like one of his mum's early album covers – two heads joined in mystic union above a rainbow, flowers sprouting from the joining of the crowns – that sort of shit. The title had been ripped away. Castro had bought the book for its cover art but he'd been rolling zeppelin joints all afternoon and cover art was ideal roach material. Around his wrist was the rubber band that usually held the whole thing together. Goog saw that it had grooved deep into Castro's flesh and was threatening to cut off his circulation and, in turn, his right hand. Castro was too stoned and absorbed in his book to notice.

In a dusty Mexican town, some guy had bumped into an Indian sorcerer. The sorcerer introduced the man to peyote and the peyote introduced the man to some pretty freaky little scenes. Goog was getting all this as the vinyl of the front seat stuck to his chin and the flat boredom of the desert droned past. He still wasn't allowed to sit in the front – Aldo's car, Aldo's rules. *Stuff him*, he thought, *I don't want to be sitting in a pool of his sweat all the way to Margaret River, anyway.*

Up ahead the road was a straight line. Where it touched the horizon, there was a pool of silver that ate the sky.

When he was seven, Goog had put a thermometer in a tumbler of boiling water, he was that type of kid. He had only wanted to see the temperature rise but the thermometer was cold and had shattered. The mercury dripped from the tumbler and slipped easily over his palm, flowing like magic. It was water *and* metal – a miracle. Goog didn't know the dangers. He was only seven, after all. With that magic trapped in a film canister, though, he was the envy of all his mates.

Aldo had broken the magic. At eight, he was just beginning his career as a bully, hassling grade twos for money and lunches. He was round, heavy and smelt like bad fruit. His fingers were thick on the magic canister, his blunt thumb quick on the lid . . .

'Spliff-time,' said Castro and ripped off another square of cover.

Goog was jerked back into the present, back to the desert and the heat-drugged flies head-butting the windows. Back to the mercury haze flooding the road ahead.

Then out of that haze a figure appeared.

At first it was merely a twist of soldering wire. Slowly it thickened to a body, with mercury gnawing at the silhouettes of legs and arms. It shimmered its way into reality like a developing print. The photo-chemicals were the sun and the blistered tar. As they got closer, Goog could see the figure was walking west, its back curved like a tree away from the road.

They were doing a hundred and twenty, the temperature

dangerously close to the red line. The Kingswood was thirsty for water and oil, the petrol was getting low too. They should have checked it in Ceduna. Now they were in the bloody desert and the Beast was dehydrating.

The figure was close now, seventy metres and closing, a dirty pack over one shoulder and one long, long finger pushed out into the road.

Castro looked up from his spliff. 'Hey, Aldo, better pick this guy up.'

Aldo nudged the Kingswood up to a hundred and twenty-five . . . a hundred and thirty.

'Aldo, we're in the middle of nowhere. How about picking this guy up?'

A hundred and forty. The thermometer needle slipped over into the red. Goog thought he could feel the heat in the car rise.

'*Aldo, stop the fucking car and pick him up!*'

'Listen, mate,' Aldo spat, 'Last time I did. Last time I listened to you and look at the fucken loser we got.'

They were doing a hundred and forty when they passed the man, flinging up dust and gravel. Goog caught a flash of something familiar – those long thin fingers, a flare of dangerous blue eyes. But at a hundred and forty it was only a moment before the man was a stick, a dot and then he was swallowed completely by rising mercury.

The sun was right overhead. Even when he pushed his shoulders hard against the door, Goog couldn't find any shade. His camera was in his lap but he was too lazy and uninspired to take photos. Off in the desert, Aldo was taking a dump, scuffing up the dull, rusty soil with the heel of his boot and crouching over the shallow hole like a wary animal. Goog watched as the wind made off with his handful of toilet paper, unfurling it and pulling it into the sky like a toilet-time willy-willy. He zoomed in on Aldo with his camera, full-frame with his pants around his ankles. A perfect album shot.

Castro was up on the road, hands on hips, staring at the horizon hopefully. Every now and then a caravan, towed by a big four-wheel drive, would barrel in from the east or west. Castro would wave like a drowning child until he could read the stickers on its jerry cans and fishing-rod holders. As it flew past, drowning him in dust and diesel fumes, he would lift his middle finger slowly and plant it in front of him like a roadside monument, making sure they got a good look in their oversized wing mirrors.

The Kingswood still ticked noisily behind Goog, the engine block cooling and contracting. Every now and then it would empty a creak into the dry air and he would imagine bad things happening beneath the bonnet. Aldo had pushed the old bus too hard. They'd never get a fanbelt out here. Should have checked it all out in Ceduna.

An old Monaro rumbled into sight and sent Castro into full-wave mode. The car rumbled up behind the Kingswood and sat there rattling like a can of stones. The roof was propped up with a tree trunk, there was no windscreen and the front quarter panels were sewn on with heavy-gauge fencing wire. Twelve eyes stared out at Goog.

The man in the driver's seat said, 'Youse blokes awright?'

'We've done a fanbelt,' replied Castro through the missing windscreen.

The man turned to a guy in the back. 'We got one in the back there, Clive?'

Clive said, 'Yep. He's here somewhere,' and grubbed around on the floor of the Monaro. He pulled up an old footy, three empty cans, a fishing rod and a Mickey Mouse mask with one ear missing. Clive showed all of these to Castro as if to say, *Will this do? Or this? What about this? Or this?*

Aldo spotted the Monaro and couldn't get his pants up fast enough. He tripped back to the highway, zipping and buttoning as he went. As he approached, his smile crashed down on his chin, flattened like a cheap imported car.

'You're Abos,' he said.

The driver didn't even flinch. He said, 'You got that right. We're the Ab-originals. The ridgy-didge-inals. That's us.'

The guys in the back laughed and slapped him on the back.

Aldo said, 'We don't need your help.'

'Yes we do, Aldo. We seriously do.' Castro smiled at the guys in the car.

Aldo spat on the ground. 'We don't need your help, awright.'

The driver frowned. 'You gotta problem, bro?' he asked.

'Look he's just a little bit colour-blind, that's all. He doesn't mean anything by it.' Castro always had the words, even in moments like these.

The driver nodded but kept his eyes on Aldo. Goog waited for something to happen, his muscles jellied with fear. There were six of them in the car. Big guys. The one in the passenger seat had a long grey beard. But before they got out, Goog would be at least fifty metres away. None of them looked like sprinters.

'Seem you do have a problem, bro,' said the driver.

Aldo's neck muscles twitched. 'I ain't your fucken bro. I got only pure White blood in my family.'

Ten eyes narrowed, ten fists bunched.

Only the driver remained calm.

He said, 'We all got red blood, bro. That's not the problem.' He pushed his leather hat back on his head so Aldo could get a good look at his eyes. 'You know what is?'

Either Aldo couldn't think of a smart-arse answer or he was scared. Whichever way, he kept his mouth shut.

'Your problem is, you've broke down . . .' The driver clicked his tongue and ran his finger around the curve of his nose. 'You've broke down aaaaand . . . you're on our laaaaand.'

He shook his head and revved the car hard a couple of times. It roared and rattled and spat oil blots as big as tin lids onto the road. He smiled at Castro and shrugged. The clutch pedal clunked up, tyres scrubbed the dirt and squealed onto the blacktop. The air was full of rubber and red dust.

Aldo screamed at the car, '*This isn't your fucken land!*' He picked up a handful of dirt and threw it down the highway. '*This is Aus-stray-li-ya!*'

Goog tossed his camera in the car. He swallowed deeply and grabbed Aldo's shoulder. 'That's enough,' he said as Aldo spun around.

Aldo opened his mouth but Castro stopped him. 'Yeah, that *is* enough, Aldo.'

It seemed like a long time before anyone came by, and even then it was only someone on foot, limping slightly.

They had passed the hitchhiker ten k's back and now he had caught up. The man had a shaved head, red raw from the sun. The grey pinstripe three-piece he wore was coated with a layer of dust and pocked with oily looking stains. He had the jacket tied around his waist, a dirty white T-shirt under the waistcoat.

'Chaps,' he said as he walked up to the car.

It was Jasper. It had been a week and almost two thousand kilometres since they had abandoned him to the cops near Lorne. There was a cut on the bridge of his nose and both his eyes were black.

Castro squinted at him and said carefully, 'Yeah, g'day Jasper. How's things?'

'Everything is fine . . . now.' He shot a look at Aldo who was kicking the car tyres as if he was going to buy the shitheap. Again. Jasper jerked his head towards the car. 'Problems?'

'Yeah. Aldo pushed the old girl a little too hard, broke a fan-belt,' said Castro.

'Wasn't my fucken fault. If youse blokes —'

'And he didn't bring a spare.' Castro was pushing him but Aldo was wary with Jasper around. He wasn't a big man but there was something big about him, and the encounter with the Aboriginal guys had shaken Aldo.

'I just happen to have the solution right here.' Jasper patted his backpack.

Castro smiled, 'All right —'

Jasper held up a hand. 'But there's a condition.'

'We don't need your fucken help, *smackie*.'

Jasper ignored Aldo, directing his attention to Castro and Goog. 'I need a lift as far as Kalgoorlie.'

'No fucken way!'

Aldo came at Jasper but Goog caught him by the arm. It didn't take much effort to hold him back.

'I am not asking *you*.' Jasper didn't even look at Aldo as he said it.

'But it's his car.' Even Goog could see that.

Aldo shrugged off Goog's grip and sneered. Jasper shouldered his pack. Taking a while to tighten the straps, he hitched it high over his hips and started off west again. He called over his shoulder, 'It is *his car*. But I have the means to get *his car* going again. It's up to you.'

'Deal!' Castro called after him.

Aldo smacked the roof of the car. 'No fucken way —'

'Shut up, Aldo!' Castro was on decisions now.

Aldo said, 'But we're not even goin to Kalgoorlie. It's too far inland.'

Castro said quietly, 'Just shut up, okay,' and then he shouted down the road, 'It's a deal!'

Jasper stopped and turned around. He walked slowly back to the car and put his pack on the ground. Without saying a word, he pushed his hand deep inside and worked his arm around – identifying objects, rejecting them, shuffling things about. When he drew out an object with his long surgeon's fingers, the guys were ready for anything.

As Jasper held it against the sky, Goog tried hard to identify it. Finally Aldo said, 'What the f—'

'This, gentlemen, is the technology that will get us on the road again.'

'Those are tights, ya fucken weirdo!'

Aldo was right. A pair of pantyhose dangled from Jasper's hand like an animal pelt. There were beads of spittle on Aldo's lips and what looked like tears in his eyes. 'Guys, he's a fucken weirdo. Probly an arse bandit or somethin. He's goin to tie us up and do us —'

'Shut up, Aldo,' said Jasper and nodded at Castro.

Aldo spat a lump of disgust onto the blacktop and started walking towards Margaret River, cracking his neck from side to side. Goog followed him with his lens until he was just a dot in the frame. Then he helped Jasper fit the tights to the engine and fan pulleys.

'Fine-quality nylon, strong and durable. It will last at least until Nullarbor. We'd probably get all the way to Perth and back.'

They were back in the car. Jasper was driving (Goog could hardly believe it) and Castro was up front with him. They had picked Aldo up two kilometres down the road. It had taken some careful negotiations to get him into the back seat, but once there, he fell asleep.

Jasper had driven them to a cattle station with a creaky windmill and a rusted fuel bowser. They had fuelled and watered the Beast and were back on the highway before Aldo woke. They drove down the middle of the road, cat's eyes lining up with the centre crease of the bonnet.

Goog pointed his lens out the window, catching the odd hawk or eagle that strayed into frame for a second or two. There was plenty of roadkill out there and the smell attracted birds and flies. It poured through the vents.

Jasper pointed at Castro's book. 'What's that you're reading?'

Castro showed him the cover, the just-over-one-third that remained. *'The Teachings of Don Juan,'* he said.

'Ah yes, Carlos Castaneda and his Yaqui Indian friend. Do you believe it?'

Castro blew through pursed lips. 'Don't really know. Spose it could've happened. It's a good story either way, the vision quests, mescalito, mushrooms. Good stuff.'

'Are you into that stuff?'

'This is the first book I've read for ages. It's okay, I guess.'

Jasper dried the palm of his right hand in front of the air vent. 'No, I mean the drugs – mushrooms, peyote?'

'Not really, it's a bit heavy for me. And who can get hold of peyote, anyway?' Castro pointed the book at the Nullarbor. 'This desert isn't exactly Mexico.'

'I have certain . . . shall we say . . . contacts. Nothing is impossible. Everything can be bought or traded.'

Jasper paused while a road train forced its way by, then continued. 'Peyote is a window. If you open it properly it will give you insights into your own soul, into the souls of other men. You need guidance though, and an ounce or two of courage.' Another road train came through, another pause. 'I'm sure you have the courage. This might seem like happy coincidence but I just happen to have some peyote on me.' He took one hand off the wheel, patted a small bag slung around his neck. 'Fancy a try?'

Goog pushed his knee into the back of Castro's seat, trying to get his attention. Jasper was a fruitloop, he was trouble.

Castro moved around in his seat. It was uncomfortable and he was sticking to it everywhere. 'Hey, if you've got some peyote, why not? I'll give it a burl.' He grinned nervously at the road, then at Jasper, then back at the road.

They drove off the highway at the spot that Ron the Beard had pointed out on the map. It seemed like a lifetime since Port Campbell, even longer since home, but the burnt black rock was there as promised. Jasper bounced the old HQ down the rough track until they caught the sharp smell of salt through the windows and felt the cool ocean breeze. Even Aldo seemed to lighten up, then. They were coastal dwellers at heart. The desert was too big, too flat, and far, far too dry.

It was getting dark when they reached the cliffs but they could hear the growl of waves beneath them. In an hour or so the moon would be up and they could check the surf. To fill in time they set up camp.

The tent had been stowed since Johanna but its mustiness had crept out of the bag and had been lolloping around the car for days. Castro voted against erecting it and rolled out his sleeping bag by the fire. Goog followed suit, scraping away the stones with his feet and laying out his board bag as a mattress. Aldo spent some time levelling the car, fluffing his pillow and unfolding his doona until it flowed out of the tailgate. Only Jasper made no attempt at preparing a bed.

'I'll cook,' he said and, gathering some saltbush and termite-riddled mulga, lit a fire. By the time the boys had finished with their sleeping arrangements, he had four plates of beans and four mugs of tea ready. He made a big show of sitting them down and handing them a plate and a mug each.

'Here you go, chaps. Bon appétit!'

Goog blew on his tea and sipped it. It was smoky and slightly bitter.

Jasper smiled at him. 'So, I expect you chaps are expecting some fair-sized waves in the morning?'

Goog took another sip. 'Yeah, well, we've heard some pretty awesome stories about this coast, hope we get ourselves some big ones.'

'I was once out in the islands,' Jasper said. 'Oahu North Shore, winter of eighty-one or eighty-two, I think it was. Waimea Bay. A friend of mine died there.'

Aldo let out a snort but Castro said, 'Shit! What was his name? We've probably heard of him.' It was unlikely. Even Castro's back issues of *Tracks* didn't go that far back.

'It's unimportant. The strange thing about that time was that a group of surfers, my friend included, decided to enlist the help of a *kahuna* to summon swell.'

'*Kahuna?*' Now Goog was drawn into the conversation. Even Aldo had turned a little to catch the words.

'The *kahuna* were a group of ancient Hawaiian priests. They had the power to summon waves, amongst other things. They knew the words to chants, what rituals to perform. Anyway, this friend of my friend found an old Hawaiian in a bar. He was just a man like anyone else, but he claimed to be descended from the ancient *kahuna*. He said his great-grandfather was the *kahuna* to the royal family. That he summoned the great waves only the king could ride. The biggest waves were *tapu* – out of bounds for commoners – and great danger befell any commoner riding them, they could even die. The spirits of the ocean would kill them.

'Well, these surfers thought wave-summoning sounded like a good way to pass a flat afternoon, so they paid the guy fifty dollars and gave him their bottle of duty-free brandy. He came back the next afternoon with an old spiral-bound notebook and a hessian sack. The surfers looked at the book and the half-drunk Hawaiian and laughed. "What's with the book, Chief?" they asked him. "This is where I write down the songs so I don't forget," he said, and took a swig from his half-full bottle of brandy. They went down to the bay and the Hawaiian, grabbing some vines out of the sack, waded into the water and began thrashing the surface with them. He started chanting, just a whole string of low vowels, a strange kind of song. Well, the bay was like a millpond, it had been for weeks. They waited. Nothing happened. They went home and bought some beers and sat on their verandah and watched the bay. Nothing.'

Jasper threw out the dregs of his tea and stared into his cup.

'Yeah? Go on.' Goog wanted the end of the story tied up neatly like it should be.

'Two days later, a big low-pressure system hit the islands. It brought twenty-five-foot waves into the bay. Only the big-wave experts went out. My friend was there.

'They pulled his body off the beach next morning. Apparently the old Hawaiian found him washed up on the sand. When they laid him out in the morgue they found strange marks on his palms. They couldn't work out how they'd got there. A girl I had occasional dealings with was a mortuary assistant down there. She went to get a camera, but by the time she got back the marks had gone.'

Goog poked at the fire with his shoe. 'So what does that mean?'

'It doesn't mean anything, Goog,' Jasper said. 'It's just a weird happening. Some things can be explained and others cannot.'

They all sat silent for a while and then Jasper pulled a piece of paper out of his jacket pocket. He unfolded it and handed it to Goog. 'Someone gave me this at a truck stop. They said they were stuck in trees and fences all down the highway, folded into little birds. Cranes. The guy said he saw an old Kingswood setting all these paper birds free.'

Goog just shrugged. Without even looking at the paper, he tossed it into the fire. It flared bright, lighting up all their faces for a moment. Then, turning black and feathery, it rose into the sky.

'You don't know anything about it? Seems like you might have been keeping bad company. You should be more careful. It can be dangerous on the road. You cross someone and next minute —' He made a movement with his hand like the explosion of a firework, his long fingers catching the glow from the fire. 'Next minute it's all coming back at you, blowing up in your face.'

Goog threw a stick at the fire. It coughed a shower of sparks. 'I don't know what you're talking about,' he said.

'I have some, shall we say, *associates* in Adelaide, who are a little concerned because they have lost something of great value to them. You wouldn't know anything about that, would you?'

Goog shook his head.

'What about you, Castro. Is your record clean? Have you been keeping out of trouble?'

Castro looked him straight in the eyes and replied, 'Look, man, if you're talking about that shit back at Lorne, well, that's between you and Aldo.'

Aldo threw his plate on the ground and walked away from the fire.

Jasper watched him go. His shaved head, dulled with a light dusting of stubble, seemed to deepen in colour. He said, 'What happened with Aldo and me was irritating, I can't deny that. Believe me, that score will be settled somehow. But I'm talking about something a little more serious.'

Castro said, 'I don't know what you're on about.' But he couldn't meet Jasper's eyes, which seemed to cloud and darken, when only minutes before they had been clear and blue.

'I'm going to get what I want. I always do,' he said.

There was a moment of awkward silence while the sound of the sea rushed up to meet them, and then Jasper stood up and nodded at Castro. 'Shall we go?'

Castro looked at him warily, 'Where exactly are we going?'

Jasper patted his suit pocket. 'Peyote. You wanted to try it. I'm ready. Are you?'

'I guess so,' said Castro meekly, getting up to follow Jasper.

The two of them walked past the circle of light thrown by the fire, out to where the moon had sucked every colour but blue from the landscape.

Goog watched them go. He didn't attempt to follow; he was tired. So tired. Eyelids were too heavy. As he lay down, he could hear Aldo snoring nearby. *Castro will be okay,* Goog told himself. *He can take care of himself.*

8

PEYOTE VISIONS

Goog lay facing the moon, his eyes flickering beneath his eyelids. Whatever Jasper had added to his and Aldo's tea was bringing on a strange dream.

In that dream, Goog could see the back of Castro's head and Jasper's face cut in half by moonlight. Jasper was pulling at the pouch around his neck, rising up and placing some small leathery buttons in Castro's hands.

'The seat of power,' said Jasper, his voice jerky with echoes.

Now Goog floated above them, the blue-black of the desert floor mapped out below. The two shadowy bodies were facing each other, their knees almost touching.

Castro put a button on his tongue. He began to chew and as he did, Goog dropped inside him. He fell in behind Castro's eyes with a jolt and immediately tasted something bitter – the peyote. He was inside Castro's head, part of Castro, sharing his thoughts and feelings.

Their mouth began to water uncontrollably. Streams of saliva wound off their chin, oceans poured from the corners of their mouth. Bitter, too bitter. All that spit drizzling from their lips. Castro chewed and chewed, jaw muscles aching with the effort.

'Spit it out, Castro.' Jasper's voice was full of thick darkness. 'Take the next button.' Jasper's eyes were blazing, his mouth twisted like a black snake.

Castro spat the mush of fibres onto the ground and put another button in their mouth. Again the bitterness. Numbness spreading over their tongue like poison.

'Do you feel the thunder?' asked Jasper.

Goog became aware of distant waves breaking over them. He could feel thunder building, a weakness in their thighs, a hollowness inside. There was sickness too, bolts of it like lightning. Flashes of it, jerking their body over the sand.

'Keep the juice inside, Castro. It is the source of wisdom.'

Jasper's face was big as a sideshow clown. Their hands felt distant and rubbery. Their spit was as thick as glue and tasted of match heads. Jasper was dancing around them, hiding the moon.

'Keep it inside.' His fingers moved like squid through the air. 'Keep it down, boy. Run towards your fears, they can only diminish. Use your fears or they'll use you.'

The stars began to drop from the sky and sand ran like water towards them. They tried to stand but their legs had gone. Castro dropped to their belly and swam over the desert floor. Islands rose around them. Seabirds fell like arrows below the sand and returned with tiny pearly fish skewered on their beaks. The black twist of Jasper's body followed them.

He taunted their slippery form. 'Dance with the devil. Sing for your supper.'

The words tore over the ocean sands, echoed from the islands. The words leaked into them, even though Castro tried to edge away. Goog could feel panic constricting them like a straightjacket.

'Run from the hunter. Pay the piper.' Jasper was the snake, smooth and deadly, winding between the rocks.

Castro said, 'I don't knowww wwhat . . . what? I . . . I . . .'

The words were as sharp as sea-urchin spines, ulcerating their tongue. This wasn't their language. Jasper was the coyote, the snake, the trickster, the tail of a desert scorpion.

'Pay the piper. Pay the piper. Pay the piper . . .'

Castro swung at the black shadow, but it was too quick and pulled back around the spinifex, came at them from another angle.

'Don't shoot the messenger. I'm only the messenger. Don't *fear* the messenger.' Jasper's eyes were shining yellow, the pupils black slices. 'Aloha, my little friend. Have a niccccccce evening,' he said, obscuring the moon as he drifted away.

With the snake gone, Castro took a deep breath. The air was like honey in their lungs. He dived beneath the desert's surface. Below, everything was branded with mackerel-striped light. Anemones clung to rocks, sucking and spitting out gritty liquid. Down Castro dived, deeper and deeper, until sand entered their ears and crushed their ribcage. He pressed fists against their temples. Up above, the moon rocked in the sky, stars and satellites collided.

Deeper down, dark shapes swung under rock shelves. Lumps of grey muscle roiled over stones. These were the magnets that Castro was drawn to. There was danger, something old and powerful about the dark shapes. Goog tried to warn him but he was slipping away from Castro, his buoyant body returning to the shining surface of the desert. Castro's fingers splayed up to Goog as he rose. His eyes were wide, full of madness, fear and betrayal.

'Goog . . . Goog . . . Goooooog!'

The voice was crumpling in from above him.

'Goog! Wake up, you dopey little shit.'

Goog's eyes opened to Aldo standing over him. Instinctively, he shielded his face.

'About fucken time,' said Aldo 'Castro's gone. Jasper too. I always said that fuck-knuckle was up to no good. He spiked our tea.'

'Castro! Caaastro!' Goog felt like a headcase, shouting so loud out here. He felt like a headcase anyway. Whatever Jasper had drugged them with had not fully left his system. It was still dark and the landscape looked fearful, cursed with shadows and strange shapes.

Aldo was off in the distance. Goog could only just hear him swearing at rocks and shouting Castro's name. Why had they trusted Jasper? How far would he go? What did he want? Every answer that Goog came up with created another twenty questions. Jasper was like a Russian doll, layer after layer opening to reveal another.

The dream was still vivid in Goog's mind. It was just a dream, had to be. But when Goog shut his eyes again, he saw Castro lying on a beach, his body covered with burnt-out stars and tangled in fishing net. Nearby, the sea was calling for him and the weeping of seagulls drifted on the wind. In his hand, Castro held a cuttlefish bone, carved with a dozen or so symbols. Castro pressed the bone until the symbols were absorbed by his palm.

Goog shook himself clear of the dream. That was all it was – a dream, full of the usual bullshit. There was no point searching for meaning; he could be there all night doing that. What was real, what was important, was that Castro was missing. Maybe Aldo and his hunches were on the money: Aldo was sure Jasper had done something terrible and that Castro was in trouble. Aldo was always so sure, no matter what the evidence. He was always confident of his view of the world, skewed as it was. Goog envied that confidence. Aldo would never be stranded when a bad tide rolled in.

The outline of an abandoned car surged out of the desert, its bulky shape appearing like a mirage. Goog could feel his arms and legs loosen with fear. He was still groggy and he knew he needed to be clear-headed. Jasper could be anywhere, waiting to do god-knows-what. As he drew nearer to the car, he could see the doors had been ripped off and someone had blown shotgun holes in the body. There were flattened beer cans all around.

Walking as quietly as the beer cans would allow, Goog was almost touching the car when a scream pulled his stomach up to his heart. It came from the inside of the wreck. A strong smell of piss hit him and he gagged. His pulse drummed in his ears, his chest hurt. *Swallow your fear, boy,* he thought, *swallow your fear.* But his fear was huge, dry; it caught in his throat.

Something burst out of the car, battering him on the head as it came. It tore at his cheek and knocked him onto his back. He rolled into a ball to protect his face from the attack, but nothing came. As he unfurled, he saw a small shape bounding into the desert.

It was some kind of cat, most likely feral, with a scream like a horror-show banshee. Goog turned away from the car, rubbing the blood from his cheek. There was a low moan behind him. This time he was closer to the noise, almost on top of it, and he knew it was human. He listened as it came again – from

somewhere beneath the car. The car was at most six inches
above the ground, the tyres were shredded like old bags and the
whole thing was resting heavily on the rims. Goog could just
see what looked like a body crammed under it. A hand lolled
out towards him and, as the moonlight caught it, Goog saw
Castro's Rip Curl watch.

The hand was cold and damp, and Goog pulled at it until
Castro's shoulder was free of the car. When he pulled again, he
could just make out Castro's hair. How Castro had wedged
himself under there was a mystery. Jasper had been up to some
weird shit.

Reaching both arms under the car, Goog worked his hands
into Castro's armpits and dragged him out slowly. The rusted
door-sills scraped at Castro's skin and sand was forced into the
necks of his boots. Goog got him clear of the car and fell onto
his back. Rising on his elbows, he looked at Castro, his hair
plastered flat against his head with sweat, both arms outstretched and the flats of his hands exposed to the moon.

There were strange marks on his right palm, symbols, white
against the red of his skin. Swirls, squiggles and what could be
letters, nothing like anything Goog had ever seen. He blinked
them away as Aldo approached.

'He's fucken gone.'

'Who's gone?' Goog didn't get it. Castro was right here.
Apparently Aldo didn't care, didn't even notice.

'That fucken weirdo, Jasper. He's gone. Trashed our gear and
pissed off. Must have done it while we were asleep, or out here.'

'It's all right. I found Castro.'

'Yeah, but that bastard Jasper —'

'Look, I found Castro. Now give me a hand to carry him back to camp.' Castro was limp in Goog's arms. When Goog tried to stand him up, his legs wouldn't hold him.

They stoked up the fire and wrapped Castro in a blanket. He had come to, but was shivering and still groggy. He kept talking about being protected, about how he was going to be all right now. How he had it all worked out. Goog stared into the fire and listened. He couldn't shake off the dream. The strangeness of it hung like woodsmoke at the edges of his vision. If he closed his eyes, he could still see Castro diving deeper and deeper, swimming down towards his fears. That was the difference between them: Castro used his fears to move ahead, Goog was trapped by them.

Aldo had all their stuff laid out on the ground and was checking what was missing. He was convinced Jasper had made off with half his tapes.

'He's after the disk,' said Castro suddenly.

'Wünderkind. He's bloody knocked off my Wünderkind, the prick.'

Goog pushed a stick into the fire, 'Aldo, you lost that tape at the start of the trip.'

Castro stood up. 'The disk. Jasper's after the disk.' He wobbled over to the car and was lost in the shadows for a moment.

Goog watched him get swallowed by the dark, heard the frantic scrabbling at the door handles. There was silence, then a door slammed. Castro returned, with relief relaxing the corners of his eyes and pulling up the edges of his lips.

'What disk? What are you on about?'

'He was after the disk. That was why he came here, to get it'.

Aldo looked up from his tapes. 'What fucken disk, Castro?'

'The disk from the Brotherhood of Aryan ResponsiBility. The Zip disk. I knocked off the cashbox and the disk was in it.'

Aldo was quiet for a second or two. The cracking of the fire and the background buzz of the surf became louder. 'You did fucken what?'

Castro's face was bright, his eyes shining. 'I took it, the disk. I tossed the cashbox, I was only after the money, but the disk was such a golden opportunity. Who wouldn't want to stuff up their plans? Those nazis are scumbags, always acting so fucking superior. Who wouldn't want to stuff the bastards up?'

'Those *bastards* were my Brothers. Are my Brothers! They took us in. They're like family to me. And now what am I supposed to do? You stole their disk and now they're going to come after us. This is because of you.'

'Wait a minute, Aldo.' It seemed unfair to Goog that Castro should carry the blame for everything.

'Yes, wait a minute.' Castro was on his knees looking at the fire. 'Jasper said something to me while we were out there.' He pointed into the desert. 'Something about him running stuff for the Brotherhood. He was their drug runner.'

'No way! No way they'd be involved with that!' Aldo was shaking his head, his fingers bunched together at his temples.

'You must have seen it, Aldo,' Goog said. 'That house of theirs – the scales and ziplock bags, the drugged-out guy, Torquil. All that talk about candy. And how come they've got so much money?'

Castro turned to Aldo, the light from the fire orange on his cheeks. 'Jasper was delivering a package – the drugs the cops found on him. The Brotherhood sold drugs to fund their operation. They fed Torquil heroin so he'd do their site.'

Goog said, 'And that means you're to blame, Aldo. You pissed Jasper off. You got him busted and in the shit with the Brotherhood. You started this whole ball rolling. By dobbing Jasper in to the cops, you betrayed your precious Brothers and now they *have* come after us. They sent Jasper.'

'Bullshit! That is such fucken crap! I wouldn't do anything to harm my Brothers. Youse are just tryin to turn this around. Well, it won't fucken work. Jasper was just a smackie, *is* just a smackie. He's fucken trouble and I said it from day one. The Brotherhood of Aryan Responsi-Bility would want fuck-all to do with a wanker like that.'

'Forget arguing over who's to blame,' said Castro. 'It could go on forever.'

Aldo threw a tape into the fire. There was black smoke and a sickening smell of plastic. He went over to the car, opened the door and sat down in the driver's seat.

Goog got up and sat beside Castro, watched a cloud of sparks rising. He said quietly, 'I guess you ditched the disk.'

Castro looked at him. 'Disk?'

'The disk you took, you ditched it, right? You haven't still got it?'

'Of course. That's what I told Jasper. I got rid of it back in Adelaide.'

'Yeah, why would you want to keep it anyway?' said Goog.

'A souvenir, to prove I did it. To make Aldo wake up to himself. Lots of reasons.'

Goog looked at Castro carefully. 'But you did ditch it?'

'Yeah, of course I did. I ditched it.'

Castro face went slack for a moment, he stared at the fire. Then his eyes went wide. 'Where's the book?' he said.

'What book?' Goog didn't know what he was talking about.

Castro was flitting between thoughts like a moth.

'My book.' Castro shouted at the car, 'Aldo, where's my book?'

Aldo leapt out of the front seat. 'What fucken book? I haven't seen no fucken book. First the disk and now the book. Leave me alone. Can't you see I'm tryin to think?' He dented the car roof with his fist, got back in and slammed the door.

Castro crawled over to the piles of clothes, tapes and food. He picked up jumpers and towels, shook them, threw them off to one side.

'My book. I need my book. My Castaneda book. I need it.'

'Look, mate, we'll buy you another one in Margaret River,' said Goog.

'The answers are in that book. He told me. The answers are there.' Castro was almost sobbing now. He stumbled over to the car, bashed at the window. 'My book, Aldo, I need my book.'

Aldo pushed the door open, throwing Castro onto the ground. He grabbed him by the shoulders and shook him. 'Your psycho mate nabbed your book along with half of our food and most of our water. Five litres we got left, we could fucken die out here. He's had the fifty bucks out of the ashtray too. Never, ever trust a smackie!' He pushed Castro's shoulders away and stamped out from the campsite towards the cliffs.

Goog hated Aldo. Hated him for all his misplaced anger and aggression. For his stupidity at getting all of them involved in this mess. He hoped Aldo would keep on walking, ahead fifty metres and down thirty. The bastard deserved it.

9

ROAD TRAINS

When Goog woke up there was still the gloomy tinge of night in the sky. Dark rags of cloud blew along the horizon, above the saltbush and ochre soil. He groped his way out of his sleeping bag and stamped the cold from his legs. The morning air hurt his lungs, his hands and his feet. The desert shouldn't be this cold. He gathered some twigs and a bunch of thin, dry grass and coaxed some life back into the campfire. Over to the east, the sun was starting to spread itself out; to the west, the moon was dropping out of sight.

Castro had crashed out in a heap nearby and Aldo's heavy shape rose and fell under his doona. Last night's evil dreaming lingered like mist. Goog looked at the old Kingswood, at its rapidly decaying body. Things were starting to fall apart badly, both with the car and the trip.

He shook his head free of it. A good surf would help them all forget. The snoozers would lose; Goog would have the first glimpse of the break.

The path was narrow, worn like a creekbed by the feet of surfers and fishos. There were signs at the clifftop warning about the dangers of standing too near to the edge and the serious things gravity could do to the human body.

Goog knew the sea was slowly pulling the cliff apart, eating the land, reclaiming lost territory. He remembered when he was eight and London Bridge (that tiny limestone island with its arm thrust out to the Victorian coast) had fallen down. The TV news showed helicopters winching panicked tourists to safety and the waves swarming over broken bits of rock. Even solid rock couldn't last forever. It was bound by the same rules of change as everything else.

He eased up to the edge of the cliff where the tufts of wiregrass were afraid to go. His camera swung from his neck like a pendulum. The sea was as smooth as newly laid concrete, and a lone albatross screeded the surface like a builder's trowel. Dad had once told him that albatrosses spent ten years at sea, drinking salt water and dreaming of land. They came back to the coast to breed. Sailors feared them, believed they caused bad luck.

A strong updraft lifted Goog's hair and made him uneasy and exhilarated. He shut his eyes and stretched his arms wide out from his sides, leaning his body into the wind, as if today would be the day when he could finally leave the ground behind.

'What the fuck are you up to?' It was Aldo, picking the night's crust from his eyes. 'You're a true fucken psycho, mate.' Aldo was back on form. Nothing seemed to disturb his world view.

Goog didn't reply. He just looked back out to where the albatross was skimming over the ocean, hungry for fish.

'Check out the left on that,' Aldo said, pointing to the foot of the cliff.

Goog had to lean his head out over his feet to see where the waves were ripping along below. His camera nearly pulled him over so he took it off and sat it by his feet.

There was no beach below, just piles of rocks as big as houses, between which the sea gnawed at stone. Fishos or surfers had roped rough, homemade ladders to the cliffs; they dropped thirty metres to a small plateau of rock. Beyond the rock lay a nice flat wedge of reef that was throwing up a beautiful peeling left-hander. It didn't look that big from this distance but Goog knew that at sea level things could be a lot different.

The ladders looked incredibly frail – three of them, like the fossilised remains of some old sea snake, wracked against the cliff. Goog wondered whether it was clever to climb down that spine with a six-foot piece of fibreglass wedged under one arm. If something happened down there they would never make it back to the top. If a ladder fell they would be stranded. If the tide claimed the rock shelf they would have to wait out in the ocean until the moon pulled the water back. These *ifs* were big, bigger than Goog's desire to surf the break. But *if* Castro said go, then they would go. And *if* Goog backed out, he would never live it down.

Castro was first down the path, yipping like an excited kelpie, bare feet skipping between the sharp little pebbles. He seemed more charged than ever, unaffected by last night's activities. When they had shaken him awake, he had bolted down two slices of bread and a banana and grabbed his board. There was no mention of Jasper, the Zip disk or the Castaneda book. No talk of peyote, abandoned cars or secret symbols.

Aldo walked ahead of Goog as if he were leading them into battle. His black eyes stared straight ahead. His brow was pulled down like a dirty bandana. Goog's feet were numb with cold but the small stones exploded under his soles like land-mines. Every step was an exercise in pain.

At the spot where the wooden ladder poked above the end of the continent, Goog drew a deep lungful of air. Castro and Aldo hadn't paused. They didn't even consider the danger. Goog thought about the dream, how Castro had dived towards the dark shapes. He strapped his legrope to his wrist, waited until Aldo started on the second ladder, then climbed away from solid ground.

The ladder swayed every time he put his foot down, flexing into the scabby layers of rock. Goog felt like he was stepping back in time. Tiny shell fossils poked out from the cliff face, stranded on a sea floor that had been thirty metres higher than it was now. He shook himself back into focus, back to the present, and gripped his board tightly as the updraft threatened to tear him into the salt-streaked air. He hooked his toes over the rungs and forced himself to breathe. One hand was holding onto his board, the other gripped the ladder. Between each step he had to let go and take another grip. This moment caused his body to burn with the fear of flight.

The second ladder of the set was thinner and wearier than the first but Goog had begun to make peace with his fear. If his mates had dragged him into this, then he had to follow through. He edged his way down. Standing on the ledge below ladder number two, he drew a breath and looked down on the back of a sea eagle spiralling on the thermals. If only his bones were hollow, then he would float on air too.

Ladder number three was about ten metres long and even

thinner than the others. The uprights were made from worm-riddled saplings, as thick as Goog's wrist near the top. The rungs were nailed and roped but in places the rope had begun to fray, and some of it hung off, swaying gently in the breeze. When Goog stepped onto the ladder, it sagged into the cliff. He looked down to the base, where Castro and Aldo were watching and waiting. Seeing him pause, Castro looked away and walked to the edge of the platform to study the break.

From where Goog clung to the ladder, the bottom still seemed a long way off. Aldo laid his board down carefully on the rock and put his hand on a rung. Goog saw him look up, saw his eyes narrow as he nudged the bottom of the ladder in towards the cliff. The bastard was pissed off about the whole Brotherhood mess and Goog was there, Goog was convenient.

A slow ripple ran the length of the ladder. Goog gripped the rungs as it shook to the top. Three small pieces of sandstone fell, narrowly missing Aldo, turning to powder on the rock shelf. This pissed him off some more and he shook the ladder again, harder this time. The ladder bucked, the top pulling free of the cliff for a terrifying moment. It hung there for a second. For two. In perfect balance. Then it clattered back against the rock. Fear and anger made Goog's grip tighter.

'Piss off, Aldo!' he shouted, but the sound of the waves drumming on the rocks drowned the sound. Even if Aldo had heard the shouts, he wouldn't have given a shit. Goog could see him smiling, rattling the ladder with his hand. Castro was still studying the break. Goog was alone.

Castro turned and shouted something but Aldo shook the ladder again, with both hands this time. Goog watched the tremor run up the rails and the ladder bend in to the cliff, hang for a second, then spring free.

His feet dropped away. His left hand lost its grip on the board and it floated off. Reaching the end of the legrope, the board jerked his other wrist, the one that held him to the rung. Hanging by one hand, muscles burning with acid, he tried to twist back towards the ladder, tried to grab hold with his other hand. The taste of fear covered his tongue, thin and sour like the lip of an old aluminium can. His fingers slipped and his ladder-arm tightened, shooting pain up through his shoulder. He grabbed again but the rung was too thin, too slippery. His shoulder ached; the muscles of his right arm were as tight as bowstrings.

His board was spinning on the legrope, tugging on his wrist. If he relaxed, there was eight metres of relief before the rock changed him forever. If he fell, there would be no saving him; he would end up bloody and broken at the bottom of a thirty-metre cliff in the middle of nowhere. Goog tried for the rung again. It took everything he had and then some, but this time he caught the rung and managed to swing back onto the ladder. He hugged it wildly, a salty tang at the back of his throat.

After a dozen deep breaths, he was able to look down again. Castro and Aldo were arguing. He couldn't hear the words but he could see the rough jerks of their heads and an angry show of hands. Castro pushed Aldo in the chest and he stumbled back a step. Recovering, Aldo shoved back. He was bulky, much heavier than Castro, and the shove folded Castro's chest inwards, until his head snapped back and his heels caught on the rock. Castro fell heavily, his head bouncing off stone. He rolled to one side and was still.

Without waiting to see if Castro was okay, Aldo grabbed his board, strapped on his legrope and jumped into the water. He paddled hard as the wave drew back, exposing the edge of the shelf and its shining folds of bull kelp. Goog waited for Aldo to be dredged over the rock, hoping he would be slammed by the next wave. But Aldo managed to dig deep and pull away. He dragged himself to the safety of deeper water and then continued slowly out towards the line-up.

Castro rolled onto his back and rose slowly to his feet. Goog saw him test his head for blood, running his hand over his scalp. He cupped his left shoulder and rotated it a couple of times. Then, grabbing his board, he waited for a surge and jumped forward into the water.

Goog looked up at the top of the cliff and then down at the eight metres left to go. He wedged his board so tightly under his armpit that it hurt and eased down the last twenty-six rungs.

The rock shelf felt slightly warm against his feet. Near the edges he could see the black thumbs of cunjevoi spitting out seawater. Castro was still paddling out to the line-up. Goog saw him stab his finger towards Aldo, who flipped him the bird in return. It was like a silent movie with the waves as background music, slapping against weathered rocks.

Aldo saw an incoming set and paddled out to meet it, turning his board at the last moment and stroking in. The wave rose up over a suck rock and launched him from the lip. He landed heavily but the speed of the wave carried his board on and he pulled it through a big bottom turn. Castro was concentrating on making it over the incoming wave. Aldo drove hard off the top and then in a big arc towards him. Castro abandoned his board and dived as Aldo's fins raked across the surface.

The shelf was only a metre or so above sea level and Goog lost sight of them in the trough of the incoming waves. As the wave in front petered out it revealed the next one in the set. It was bigger, six foot maybe. When Castro surfaced, he saw it coming. Goog could make out the rise in his shoulders as he sucked in a huge gulp of air. The wave was breaking, barrelling over the reef. Castro went under. He was out of sight for a long time as the wave roared over the shallow reef. It seemed small compared to the day at *Elephants* but it was packed with raw energy. The lip pounced on the sea and folded up on itself. It snarled and spat foam.

Goog walked to the edge of the shelf, where Castro and Aldo had been fighting earlier. Scanning the break he eventually saw Castro bob up like a cork. Pulling in his board by the legrope, Castro dragged himself onto it and managed to push over the next wave. Goog lost him again in the trough.

In the intermission Goog felt something soft and spongy beneath his toe. He bent down and picked up a small triangle of blue neoprene from Castro's wetsuit. Then he saw the blood – a thin film of it on the barnacles and some deep red blotches on the rock itself.

Goog shaded his eyes and squinted out to where Castro had made it to slack water. There was a ruffle on the surface beyond him that could have been a shoal of fish or the rising of water over a bommie. Only there was no shoal of fish and the bommie was off to Castro's right.

The last wave of the set hit the cliffs and there was silence. It was as if the noise had been sucked away, no blunt thunder of waves, no seagull cries. The air seemed full of static, the sky was sliced by sharp clouds.

Goog saw the triangle of fin rushing towards Castro. Another set began to rise. The fin rose as well, climbing out of the sea, pushing up water as it went. The thing was huge; it was unstoppable. They had heard all the stories (from the fishos, the Beards back at Port Campbell, the drunk in the pub only two days ago) but they had been only stories. Goog could see Castro's frantic paddling, the shape rising out from black water to meet him and the wave running before it. The wave slipped under Castro and he clawed in desperation at its face. It was too small and Goog could see it wasn't going to break in time to save him. The shark was below the waterline, invisible to the naked eye. Castro lost the wave and Goog watched as it obscured him.

Aldo was back on land, his face slapped silly with disbelief. Goog spotted him and realised what had happened. He had seen the shark and paddled in. He had left Castro alone out there. Aldo, for all his big talk, was a coward. Goog, for all his cowardice, would need to be the hero.

Goog flung himself at the water and stroked hard for the spot where Castro and the shark had been. The ocean was flat, foaming still from where the set waves had churned its surface. Out at the suck rock, he found the tail of Castro's board, the legrope neatly sliced off near the end. He paddled round, diving, opening his eyes underwater, where his fears swam in dark circles. But there were only flakes of fibreglass and the endless motion of the sea.

Castro was gone.

Goog climbed back on his board and lay there for a while. The birds returned and he watched numbly as the albatross scoured the sea. He felt nothing. He hit his head on his board to see if he could still feel pain. Bashed it again and again until the tears came. He began to sob – huge, rough, body-jarring sobs. He didn't care if sharks swarmed up from the depths, their sensitive noses picking up vibrations that flowed through the water like sound. So what if they came, with their sharp bright teeth and sandpaper skins? He'd kill them. Pull out their eyes with his fingers, rip their gills, choke them as he slid into their throats. He arched his neck back and gagged on tears, nausea washing inside him. Pressing his ear to his board, he listened to the slapping of the ocean. He looked across the blisters of wax to Aldo, cowering below the cliffs.

Hate gave him the strength to paddle in.

It was dark when they got a fire going, a half-hearted attempt that gave off little heat. They had wasted the day staring out to sea, trying to conjure up Castro from the peaks and valleys of waves.

The great white was still swimming down there, digesting the remains of Castro. Castro, the bloke who would live forever. The one in three guaranteed to squeeze everything he could out of life. The one who faced his fears and lost.

The fire gave them a focus, a reason not to talk. A car rumbled up the track. By firelight they could read the driver's door – *E&E Lamb, Roo Shooters* – and see a crude cartoon of a smiling kangaroo with a rifle in its paws.

The Lambs had a mobile phone and a couple of brand new 22s on the back seat, a case of beer in the boot and the half-cured scrotums of forty-seven kangaroos. They had no reply to tears, no comfort for sadness. They would never see Goog and Aldo again and were glad of it. Eric handed Goog his mobile and told them they should report the attack to the police in Eucla. Goog walked into the dark and pretended to call while Ed quietly reamed the barrel of his gun. There was no way Goog could talk to the police yet, there was too much to tell, too much pain involved. The Lambs left as soon as they could, giving them a can of Emu Ale to share and a business card:

E&E Lamb Roo Shooters Pty. Ltd. They had only come for a spot of fishing. They didn't need any of that weird shit.

Goog walked over to the top of the cliff and lobbed the can over. He watched it arc down to the rock shelf and split open like a ripe melon. He held his camera in his other hand and thought about tossing it too. Life had become too real, too painful to photograph.

Back at the fire, Aldo pulled out a bottle of Beam he'd been hiding in his duffle bag and passed it to Goog. Still staring at the fire, Goog slowly unscrewed the cap and threw a rough shot of warm whisky down his throat. It burned, bringing tears to his eyes. His stomach started a protest. He passed the bottle back.

Aldo said, 'That Jasper has somethin to do with all this. He's trouble. I said it from day one.'

Goog nodded. Jasper was trouble but Goog didn't know where he fitted into Castro's disappearance.

Aldo swallowed another mouthful. 'We should keep fucken goin, y'know. We need to get to Margarets.'

'No. We've got to wait and see if Castro comes back.' Goog was numb with pain; the bourbon didn't even touch the sorrow.

'Shit, Goog, you saw that thing. It was huge. Castro isn't comin back.'

Goog knew it was true. He had sat there all day wishing it wasn't but no amount of wishing would bring Castro back.

Aldo said, 'We owe it to Castro to keep goin.'

The fire flared-up, reddening Goog's face. 'You owed it to Castro to save him from that shark. You owed it to him not to bounce his head off the rocks!'

'That wasn't my fault.'

'And whose fault was it? Whose fault has it been all along,

Aldo? Castro's dead and I reckon it's your fault.' Goog's finger was straight out, spearing Aldo's heart.

Aldo's head was turned at a strange angle, his mouth was distorted. 'What about you? We had the fight coz of you!'

Goog jumped up, fists bunched tight. He flew at Aldo and smacked him in the face. Blood burst from Aldo's nose. He sat there stunned, swaying, his hand cupped over his mouth and nose, blood oozing from between his fingers. Goog had never hit him before, he had never hit anyone. This was a trip for firsts.

'Come on, you cowardly fuck. Get up and fight.' Goog stood with his fists raised and the great sweep of sky behind him. 'Get up!'

'Mate, it wasn't my fault,' Aldo said into the palm of his hand.

'He was bleeding because of you. You never even tried to help him.' Goog tried to hold the anger but he felt it leaking away and the pain returning. He could taste the salt of his own tears.

'What could I do? It was a shark. There was nothin I could do. I'm sorry. I'm sorry.' Aldo gripped his nose between his finger and thumb. He held out the open bottle of bourbon to Goog.

The apology sat strangely on Aldo's tongue. Goog couldn't even enjoy watching him grovel. He grabbed the bottle and flung it on the fire. It broke and pissed out a thin blue flame.

'I don't want anything from you. Take your fucking car and keep driving, but don't expect me to come with you.'

Goog turned his back on Aldo and walked over to the cliff. The moon washed over the desert, picking up the frosted green of the saltbush, putting the dingoes and the big reds on full alert. The path to the cliff shone like a river as Goog scuffed his way over to the cliff's edge. He leant heavily on the danger sign and dropped a stone over into the ink below. Even the moonlight was boycotting the break. The rocks and the waves were draped in funeral black but Goog thought he could hear the chunks of Castro's board rattling against the cliff. Further out, where the shark still swam with Castro deep in its belly, the sea was glazed like snow. Goog wondered how long it would take a shark to digest a human. *I'm going mad,* he thought. He felt as though there were pieces of him flying outwards like a broken mirror; he felt as if someone had scissored him into small flakes and he would never fit all the bits back into their proper places.

Castro was gone. He would have to say it out loud to make it real. 'Castro is gone.' Under the ocean was eighteen years of energy, under the ocean that wrapped its way round the continent and washed up at Margaret River. Further up it pushed onto coral reefs and sand islands – Flores, Sumba, Sumbawa, names like a mantra that would bring Castro back.

Aldo was right and how he hated him for it. They had to go on. It would be pointless turning back now. For Castro, if nothing else, he would put up with Aldo. For another fifteen hundred odd kilometres he would stomach the bastard. For Castro. And to prove to everyone else that he could finish something.

Goog heard Aldo scuffing down the path towards him. About three metres away Aldo stopped and stood in the middle of the path, blood from his nose smeared over his right cheek.

'Mate, I dunno why I did it. Sometimes I just do things.' His big red hands were hanging at his sides; he looked like a sad child. 'I know I should have tried to help him but I was scared. I should have helped him. I loved him too y'know.' He stumbled over *loved* like it was French. Or maybe Indonesian.

Goog didn't reply. He just turned and walked back to the car. Without stopping or turning to look at Aldo he said, 'We'll leave tomorrow morning.'

WEST

10

TOGETHER ALONE

A hundred kilometres west of Eucla, Aldo spoke up. He was in the passenger seat, hunched and weary.

'Y'know I don't wanna be like this.' He sounded as if had been choosing these words for a while.

'Like what, Aldo?' Goog ran his right hand around the steering wheel and edged the Kingswood up to ninety.

'Y'know, like I am.'

Goog didn't know what to say. The seat had suddenly become lumpy and the wind was blowing hair in his eyes.

'Guess no one really likes me.'

'Well, Aldo, you don't make it easy for people.'

'I know I fu—- I can't help myself sometimes. Words come out wrong. I feel angry all the time.'

'You just have to lighten up a bit. Stop being so hard on everyone.'

'Yeah.' Aldo reached for a cigarette but slumped back in the seat, as if the effort was too much. They both sat still and quiet for a while, listening to the whistle of the wind and the hum of the road. Then Aldo said, 'I got no one, y'know. No one.'

'Look, mate, I just want to drive, okay. We've got a long way to go.'

More silence. More road.

'Where we goin?'

'Margaret River.'

'Yeah, but where tonight?'

Goog looked at the fuel gauge. 'Norseman probably.'

'No one, mate. You know how alone I feel?'

This desert was too big, too empty.

Goog said, 'You got your family. You got Saxon.'

'My family, they're not . . .' He trailed off, pinched his lips together with his big dirty fingers.

'Well, Saxon then. Dogs are always there for you.'

Looking out the side window, Aldo said, 'Saxon's dead.'

'No, Aldo. You left Saxon with your brother-in-law.'

Aldo rubbed his nose with the flat of his palm. 'My sister hates dogs. She hates me. Most of all me. I couldn't leave him there.'

'It doesn't matter where you left him. He'll be there when you get home.' Goog hated where this was going.

'No, he's dead! Fucken dead, Goog!' Aldo smashed his hands down on the dash.

Goog swerved onto the other side of the road, corrected, and got the Beast back over.

'I killed him, Goog. Had him put down. Didn't want to have the worry of him while I was away.' Aldo's eyes were red and watery and his nose had begun to ooze blood. 'I killed him, Goog. He was the only mate I had.'

'What about me and Castro?' Goog wished he could have pulled the words back.

'Fuck! You, mate? You? You hate my guts. I know ya do. And why the fuck not. After what I done. First Marcella and then Castro.'

Goog had almost started to feel sorry for him but the mention of Marcella wiped that out. 'Don't bring Marcella into this. Don't even mention her name.'

'I couldn't believe a chick like that would want a guy like me. It was a fucken miracle . . .'

'Shut it, Aldo!' Without Castro things were getting out of control.

'She was so soft. So nice to me. Couldn't believe it.'

Goog lost his position on the road for a while and had to fight the car back onto the blacktop. 'Aldo, if you don't shut your fucking mouth right now I'm going to do it for you.'

Aldo just looked at Goog and smiled a lobotomised smile. 'She didn't want me. She wanted to get back at you. She told me after. Told me that you didn't care about her. Told me that this would make you notice. You had her, mate, and you just didn't care. I never got that. A bloke like me could wait forever for a girl like that and you got her and you just pretend like she's nothin.'

'What are you trying to do here? Are you trying to make yourself feel better? Look what you did! I was supposed to be your mate.' Goog was snatching quick looks at Aldo as the road blurred up to meet them.

'I was willing to risk it.'

Goog slammed the steering wheel. 'Fuck you!'

'I'm already fucked. You see, I got nothin now. They even told me when I left work that they wouldn't hold my job open for me. I got nothin, nothin to lose.'

'Bu—'

'No job, no girl, no mates, and my family, now there's a huge fucken joke. Uncle Dougie was the only one ever gave me any time. And there was the Brotherhood, but that's fucked for me now, too. I loved Castro, y'know? Loved him. He could be a pain in the arse, but I loved him. I never wanted him to die. Everything I touch dies.'

Goog felt sympathy edging out his anger. 'Why were you so keen to stay in Torquay if there's nothing there for you? We nearly had to drag you away.'

Aldo wiped his nose on the back of his hand and looked at the streak of blood. 'I *know* Torquay. If I go somewhere else, things'll be just as bad. Worse even.'

'Just shut up for a while, Aldo. Try to get some sleep.'

Goog wound the window down further until it dropped out of its tracks and landed with a thunk in the bottom of the door. Soon the road noise lulled Aldo into an uneasy sleep. He kept batting imaginary flies away with his hands and mumbled softly to himself. The day started to heat up, not real hot by Nullarbor standards, but enough to give a watery shimmer to the road ahead.

Goog's eyes were burning. He found that by shutting them tight they would cool for a moment. He began to think he could see through his closed lids, sense the road ahead like some zen master. But it was just the endless ribbon of tar imprinting itself onto his irises. If there had been a corner, he would have been stuffed.

In Torquay everyone would be talking about them. They probably had the news of Castro now. The Lambs would have talked to the cops in Eucla; there was probably a warrant out for them. Mum would be worried.

But what about Marcella? Would she even give a shit? Aldo was right, Goog hadn't cared enough about her. But Aldo only knew half the story, he didn't see the pressure she put him under. If he went back to her, it would mean playing by her rules. Goog knew he had to do something, he just wasn't sure if he wanted the life Marcella had planned. It was too much to think about right now.

The road kept coming, kilometre after kilometre. He watched the odometer clicking over. Lines running up towards the car. The hum of tyres on tar. Just shut his eyes for a moment. Heavy eyes. Let them drop like a curtain on the white-hot light.

Aldo was weeping on the roadside, his lap full of blood. There was blood rubbed over his cheek and into his hair. His head had not been shaved since home. The hair had grown quickly, like desert grass, so his flaking scalp was almost hidden.

'Death is following me,' he sobbed to himself.

A cut across the bridge of his nose had leaked a thin red line down to his chin.

The car was a mess – front quarter panel pushed in against the tyre, headlight opened up like a plucked eye. The grille was shattered and the fins of the radiator were filled with locust corpses and struggling beetles.

'Death is following me!' Aldo said again, louder this time, more real. He clawed at his throat and left a thick paste of blood around his Adam's apple. There were already two kites circling above him, the beneficiaries of road deaths. They hung in the thermals thrown up from the road, their heads cocked to one side then the other, waiting for life to be pronounced extinct.

Goog opened his eyes and looked at the crown of Aldo's head. He could see the thick pulsing of blood through a vein behind his ear.

'Leave it alone, mate,' he croaked. *God, he felt so sick. So totally alone.* 'Leave it.'

He had his camera in his hands. There was a red smear over the lens and just looking through it made him feel ill. Far from protecting him from the world, it framed his fears, the disgust he felt for the scene in front of him. It magnified everything, zoomed in and exaggerated the small, disturbing details: the feather stuck to Aldo's cheek, the thread of blood slipping from the eagle's beak.

Aldo hugged the eagle's body to him as Goog tried to lift it. It was massive and angular, the wings open and twisted. Aldo rolled his body around it like a sheath so there was no way Goog could prise the corpse free. The wings were awkward. They wouldn't fold in like Aldo wanted them too. The beak was pressed hard into his navel.

Aldo started rocking.

'Death . . . death . . . death . . . death . . .' he said over and over.

The wedge-tail had been tearing at a flattened rabbit corpse when they came across it. It tried to rise from the road, a slow and improbable take-off. Its right wing had caught the grille, dragging the eagle into the pressed-metal guard. The road was a hunting ground and cars were predators.

Aldo had red dirt and downy feathers on his neck. 'Deeeaaaaaath . . .' He had placed feathers around him in a circle and painted bloody symbols on the rocks around him.

Goog shivered at the memory of Castro's symbols, the ones on his palm that had seemed so real. If Castro were here now, he would know what to do. *How could Castro have left him alone with Aldo? Why did Castro have to die?* Goog had all the questions but no answers.

That seemed to sum up his entire life.

An hour passed. Cars slowed to see what was up but when

the drivers noticed Goog's worried eyes and Aldo's insistent rocking, they stomped on their accelerators, leaving a cloud of dust and the rotten-egg smell of unleaded fumes. Goog thought about leaving Aldo but Castro's memory and the importance of finishing this trip made him stick around. Eventually the fear of approaching dark made Aldo get up from his roadside shrine and get into the car.

He insisted on taking the dead bird. The dead bird brought a hundred flies that were silenced only when night fell. Just as the buzzing stopped, road trains and roos appeared. Their car, with only one headlight, was forced off the road by oncoming trucks and the roos showed them no respect. Goog had to slow to a crawl and beep them off the road.

The night was cold and the driver's window was missing, lost inside the gullet of the door. Goog didn't want to fix it in the dark, so he wrapped himself in his sleeping bag and kept on driving.

Aldo was fast asleep by the time they got to Norseman.

Morning in Norseman was a slow affair. The sun ambled up onto the highway, scratched itself against the roadhouse and wobbled off into the desert. The feral donkeys that had kept up their braying all night flopped onto the sand and fell into blissful sleep. Goog pushed Aldo onto his side of the car and pulled his sleeping bag over his head to escape the drone of flies.

While Aldo went over to the Caltex to order breakfast, Goog had a go at fixing the car window. There was no way he was going to spend another cold night driving or another morning hiding from flies.

He pushed a screwdriver in behind the window-winder to

release the clip that held it on. As he levered the clip, it sprang out and over the carpark. He tried to follow its path, holding his head on one side to listen for the tinkle on the ground. But the clip evaporated. Goog decided he could live without it and poked a Phillips head into the screw that held the door handle. After removing it, he pulled at the door panel. It came off easily but in two pieces. He skimmed the broken halves under a nearby truck. Now he could get at the window. As he sat on the hot tar and considered his next move, he noticed something red behind the glass.

To get to the red object he had to set the window back in its tracks. This took a fair quantity of effort and a reasonable amount of self-control and patience, things that were in short supply that morning. Eventually he forced it back into place, pushed on the winder (minus clip) and wound the window back up.

Now Goog could see it in the window cavity – a square of oddly familiar red plastic, about a hundred millimetres across. Using an old chopstick from the toolbox, he flipped the square until he could scissor-grip it with his fingers.

Goog thought back three nights, to what Castro had said about the Zip disk. *That's what I told Jasper. I got rid of it back in Adelaide.*

Well, obviously not.

Sliding the square of red plastic over the table to Aldo, Goog took a sip of his *bottomless tea*. He didn't know about *bottomless*, his cup tasted it as if it'd had someone's arse parked in it overnight.

Treating the Zip disk like a venomous snake, Aldo pressed

himself back in his seat. Goog pushed it closer, so he could see the swastika on the label. Aldo reached out and edged it off the table with his teaspoon but Goog managed to catch it in midair.

Aldo hissed, 'Take it away.'

'We can give it back to the Brothers if you want to, Aldo. It can all be over. They'll take you back. You'll be a hero. You return their Zip and you'll be the bloody hero.' Goog was working against everything he believed, against what Castro had wanted. But Aldo was heading downhill and Goog needed a handbrake badly.

'I don't want it, Goog.'

Aldo stubbed a slice of toast into his egg yolk. He had seemed brighter this morning, almost as if he had forgotten the day before. And the day before that.

Goog could see he was only making things worse, so he pocketed the Zip disk.

The counter lady eyed them with suspicion as she came over and refilled their cups. One of them was covered in blood and the other, barely a man himself, was acting like his father. She finished pouring and stepped past the display rack of chips and soft porn to her other breakfast customer, a smart chap in a three-piece suit. The suit was dirty but way too good for these parts. She started filling his cup. His hand wrapped around the china, the longest fingers she had ever seen. She followed his arm up to his neck, over his raw, shaved head and to his eyes. They were piercing blue and as cold as a glacier lake. She had worked here for twenty years and seen losers and loonies come and go but this one seemed dangerous. The tea flowed out of the cup, ran over the formica table and onto his trousers. Amazingly, he kept calm, didn't cry out or abuse her, even though the tea was hot, just off the boil.

'I'll go and get a cloth, sir,' she said, but he just nodded as if it didn't matter to him. He seemed to be listening to something. No one could be that interested in the *Chariots of Fire* muzak.

Aldo drained his bottomless cup, happier with the Zip disk out of sight. 'Down to Esperance this morning?'

Goog looked out of the window at the trucks filling up with diesel. 'Look, there's been a change of plan.'

Aldo's brow furrowed up. The plan had been Norseman-Esperance-Albany-Margaret River. That had been the plan.

'We're going to Kalgoorlie,' Goog continued.

'But that's the wrong direction. We're goin to Margaret River, Goog.' Aldo looked into his cup as if expecting a magic refill.

Goog said slowly, evenly, 'Kalgoorlie first, then Margaret River.'

'No use tryin to fool death. Death can follow us anywhere,' Aldo said cheerfully.

'Fuck death, Aldo. Will you just forget about death for one moment? Death is not following us.'

The counter lady, back behind her counter, rested her hand on the telephone.

Aldo just looked at Goog like he was the village idiot and stuffed the remainder of his toast into his mouth. 'Another cup?' Aldo asked, spraying breadcrumbs over the table.

Goog looked at the evil stain on the inside of his cup and shook his head. As Aldo moved towards the counter, Goog grabbed his duffle bag from under the table and rummaged until he found the card. *Kalgoorlie-Boulder – Gold Capital of Austra—*. The rest of the letters had been eaten by Blu-Tack and age. The image was shot from above, probably from a cherry picker, Goog thought, or a kite-mounted camera with a remote shutter release. There was a rough arena built of rusting roof iron. Outside, an unlikely blend of work utes and tourist buses were parked. Inside, it was packed with people. All heads were turned towards the camera, but not looking at the lens. Their focus was two small glints of light, coins, in the middle distance. Down on the ground a man in a dirty Akubra held a flat wooden stick in one hand. Two-up was everyone's game and Goog's dad had been no different.

Goog turned the card over:

Greg. Made it here yestday. No work so far. Kiss Priya
for me. You should see the mine its huge mate!! Take care
of your Mum and Priya. You're the man now!
Dad.
PS No surf for miles.

He had kept that card for eight years. It had been stuck on more walls than Goog could remember. After they lost their old house, the one with the jacaranda big enough to build a cubby in, they had done the rounds of the relatives. Nine different houses, none of them theirs. Dad hadn't even said goodbye. One fucking card in eight years and a long-distance phone call on his eighteenth birthday.

Aldo arrived back with his tea. 'What's that?'

Goog stuffed the card back into his bag and said, 'I'm going to pack.' As Aldo tried to gulp down his hot tea, he added, 'Just take it easy. I'm not going to leave you here.'

Back at the car, he slipped the Zip disk back into the door. Then he pulled out all the gear and began to sort it. He came up against the sorrowful reminders of Castro – his sleeping bag, his pack. The bundles of his socks made Goog want to cry. He shoved it all into a far corner of the wagon and ordered his and Aldo's stuff around it. Then he remembered the eagle.

It was rigid in the foot well of the passenger seat. Aldo had managed to fold away its wings, but it was huge. Its blood had thickened on the floor, trapping most of the flies from the night before, but the rest had called in reinforcements and were jostling for position on the carcass. Goog stifled the urge to puke and pulled the animal out by the tail. He dragged it across the carpark and hid it behind a bulk-ice freezer. Back at the car, he used Aldo's towel to scrub the worst of the blood away.

Aldo came out as he was disposing of the towel. He was munching on a piece of toast and smiling idiotically. When he saw the empty foot well, he stopped dead.

'What have you done with the eagle? That was my bird, Goog. He was mine.' Tears began to film across his eyes. 'My bird, Goog.'

Goog got in the car and turned the engine over. By this time, Aldo was on his knees in the carpark. The engine fired and Goog revved it hard, forcing out a huge cloud of oily smoke. Aldo looked up, his eyes red, his mouth distorted with grief. Goog revved again but Aldo didn't move. He rolled the car back and, leaning over, opened the passenger door.

'Get in.' Aldo just looked at him. 'Get in, Aldo!' Aldo's shoulders were humping like a pair of street hounds. 'Get in or I'm leaving you here!' Aldo buried his face in his hands.

Goog slammed the door and reversed the car at full throttle. The tyres screamed as he swung it around. He crunched it into first and peeled out to the highway. In the rear-view he could see Aldo slumped over on his side in the carpark. The counter lady was standing by the door with her hands on her hips. Behind her back, the man in the suit was pushing his long fingers into the till, snaking out tens and twenties and stuffing them in his suit pocket.

Goog made the highway and struck out for Kalgoorlie. *Fuck him*, he thought, *I'm better off alone*. He made five k's, the window rattling out some kind of code. At ten k's there seemed to be too much road ahead, endless lines and bloated corpses.

He chucked a U-ey and blasted his way back to Norseman. Aldo was weeping near the ice freezer. He had found the carcass and was cradling it in his lap. Goog packed both of them, and their following of flies, into the car. After flipping a finger at the counter lady, he got into the driver's seat and headed out with the steadily climbing sun beating in on him.

11

GOLD DUST AND BULL DUST

Goog had no idea where the two-up school was and only half an idea why he needed to go there. It was a good job that Aldo wasn't in the mood for twenty questions. The pub seemed as good a place as any for directions and Kalgoorlie seemed to have its fair share of pubs. Goog chose *The Bottom Pub* because he liked the double-storeyed front, the small dark windows and the unimaginative name.

It was just past one when he and Aldo opened the front door. Forty pairs of misty eyes swivelled round as they walked in. Twenty hands grabbed for glasses. The barmaids were wearing only bras and undies and running frosty glasses of beer and double Bundy-and-cokes over the bar. Aldo still had his I-ran-into-an-eagle-on-the-highway-and-all-I-got-was-this-lousy-T-shirt on. After two days he smelt like a backyard butcher.

'Whatcha want?' The barmaid's nipples sat neatly on the bar as she leant forward to talk to them. Aldo's jaw fell open.

'Two pots, thanks.' It was better, Goog thought, if he did the talking. Aldo and reality were not cooperating.

The barmaid crossed her arms over her nipples. 'You blokes must be from Victoria.'

Goog detected a slight accent, English maybe? 'We're from Torquay.'

She looked at the tan marks around Goog's wrists and neck. 'Surfers, eh?'

Goog nodded, ran his hand through his dirty hair. He just wanted a beer and directions to the two-up school.

'Bit far from the water here. Going out west?'

'Yup.' She still hadn't moved to get the beers, obviously not interested in making employee of the month.

'Been to *Cactus*?'

That surprised Goog. Most of these hodads wouldn't even recognise a break, let alone be able to name one. *Cactus* wasn't exactly a secret spot but it wasn't part of the regular tourist route either. It had been spotlighted a while back because of a bad shark attack; that was how this woman would have heard of it. *Ladders* belonged in the same stretch of water, the same family of breaks.

The memory of Castro was dredged up again; Goog swallowed and looked at the ground. 'Can we just get a beer, thanks?'

'Friendly bastard, aren't you? Just trying to make conversation.'

She pulled two beers and grabbed a ten-dollar bill out of Goog's hand. After she slammed the change down, she walked over and started talking to a bald man with a tiger tattooed above his right ear, who was slumped at the corner of the bar. The man looked up from his beer and smiled at Goog, his false teeth dropping to reveal the startling pink of his gums. Goog looked away and realised Aldo was no longer beside him.

There was a pile of dollar coins on the pool table but Aldo, ignoring all the rules and the chalkboard full of names, grabbed a cue from the rack. He chalked up and broke into the game in progress. The two singlet-clad players watched as he leant over the table and sank an easy ball into the corner pocket. Aldo was covered in blood and as dusty as the desert itself. The singlets looked at each other and back towards the weirdo.

From the safety of the bar, Goog watched the singlets giving Aldo the once-over. He noticed their backs tense, the muscles in their forearms tighten, their fists bunch like rocks. The burden of Aldo was too much, it was like having a nineteen-year-old child who was big, ugly and unruly. A child that people wanted to punch.

Goog moved quickly and quietly over to the pool table. He came up behind Aldo and cupped the end of the cue with his hand as Aldo was on the backstroke of his next shot.

Aldo twisted his head over his shoulder. 'Uh?' he said.

'Time to go, Aldo,' said Goog and waved a white-flag smile at the singlets.

Aldo stood upright and rested the butt of the cue on the ground.

The smaller of the two singlets had arms like twists of beef jerky. He walked over and stood in front of them. He smiled, a bad-toothed, beery smile, and pinched the tip of Aldo's cue between his thick finger and thumb. Aldo smiled back. Goog sucked in a breath of smoky air and prepared himself for fight then flight. Aldo's hand dropped from the cue. He showed his palms to the singlet and then, turning his back on him, bent down to the cube of chalk hanging from the table. He brought his nose to it and smelled it carefully. Satisfied it was what he wanted, he ripped it off its string and stuffed it into his pocket.

The room went quiet. The bald man at the bar, the one with the tiger tattoo, began to whistle. Aldo looked him straight in the eye. His nose was blue from the chalk. The tip of his tongue appeared, then more, until he looked like a Maori warrior. The bald man stopped whistling. Aldo nodded at him and walked from the room, happy, proud, confident and totally batshit crazy. Goog followed, sideways, nervous as a sheriff leaving a bad-ass saloon. As he hit the clear air, a glass slammed into the door.

Outside, the day was full of dust and bright light. A man was loading scuba tanks into the back of a ute.

He looked up at them. 'G'day.'

'G'day.' Goog was now in even less of a mood for conversation.

The man said quickly, before they had time to pass, 'You guys new in town?'

All these conversations started out the same. If only he had tape-recorded answers for these stupid questions. Goog wanted to keep moving but Aldo turned and looked hard at the scuba tanks. He had chalked two parallel lines over the bridge of his nose and beneath his eyes.

The man looked at Aldo warily and asked again, 'New in town?'

'We're new all over,' Aldo replied.

Goog thought it best to add, 'Torquay. Near Melbourne.'

'No shit, I'm from Geelong. Lived there twenty-five years, same as life imprisonment . . . but not as interesting.' The man fiddled with the pressure gauge on one of the tanks.

'We're on our way to Margaret River, just thought we'd drop in and see the two-up school. My dad used to live here.'

The man continued fiddling with the tap, tapping his nail on the glass of the gauge. 'Well, lots of blokes used to live here. Some still do.'

'My dad left. I just thought I'd like to take a look at where he lived.'

'Sweet. Why not? Free country.' He hoisted the tank up and strapped it to the back of the ute.

'What's with the tanks?' Goog was curious. Kalgoorlie was plenty far from the ocean.

The man lifted another tank, began again with the gauges. 'Divers, are ya?'

'Nup. Surfers.'

The man nodded. Water was common ground. 'Hector,' he said. No second name, just an outstretched hand.

'I'm Goog and this is Aldo.' Goog thumbed over to Aldo, who was sitting on the kerb and licking his chalk.

Hector ignored Aldo, which made a lot of sense, and said, 'Goog! Goog as in chook-egg goog? Hard on the outside, soft on the inside?'

'Yeah. Chook-egg, that's me.' Goog couldn't look at the guy when he said this. It made him feel small. But Hector didn't seem to notice.

'Sweet. So you guys ever been diving?'

'Nup.'

Goog knew there wasn't any water for miles. Hector hoisted up the tank he had been fiddling with and strapped it beside the other one.

'I'm going out past the two-up,' he said, 'Gutta meet some-one. If yez want a lift, you can jump in.

Goog bent down to Aldo and whispered, 'How about it?'

Aldo looked back to their car. 'Can't leave me bird here, Goog.'

Massaging his temples, Goog said, 'Fuck the bird, Aldo. Forget it, will you.'

'Can't leave it, Goog. Can't leave it.'

Hector was in the ute waiting. Goog grabbed Aldo's shoulder. 'Come on, Aldo, the bird will be okay. It needs a little rest, it's probably sleeping right now.'

'Don't try and trick me, Goog.'

Aldo stood up and began to walk back to the Kingswood. Goog poked his head inside the cab of the ute and said, 'Can you give me two minutes? I just got to sort something out.'

'Two minutes mate, no more, hokay?' Hector furrowed up his big forehead. 'I gutta meet someone.'

Aldo was sitting in the gutter, cradling the dead eagle, when Goog arrived at the Kingswood. Goog grabbed his camera and locked all the doors. He squatted beside Aldo.

'Not leavin him, Goog! I'm not.' Aldo crouched over the animal protectively.

'Well, bring it then, Aldo! Bring the festy piece of meat. Just come, that's all.'

Goog dragged Aldo to his feet and pushed him towards the ute.

Hector could smell the bird before he saw it and by the time he saw it, his impression of Aldo's pet hadn't lifted much.

'What the fuck is that?' he said.

'It's a dead eagle.' This sounded so Monty Python that Goog wanted to laugh.

'Well, it's goin in the back and he is too.'

Aldo climbed over the side of the ute without saying anything and propped himself against the tanks. Goog got in the cab and rattled his feet into a nest of bourbon-and-cola cans. The flat surface of the dash was covered in phone numbers, rubbed into the dust by Hector's big blunt fingers. There was a kangaroo's paw hanging from the rear-view mirror.

'That's me luck,' said Hector, pointing at the roo paw. 'Hit the bastard doing a hundred and sixty, just about totalled me.' He scooped up a couple of cans from the floor, 'Muvver's milk?' He handed Goog a Jim Beam, reached out the window and hooked one backwards onto the tray beside Aldo, scooped again and got another for himself.

Goog opened his can and took a gulp: it was warm, sour and sticky. Not exactly the perfect drink. Hector started the car and hooked a turn in the street.

'You guys stayin long?'

'No, probably only till tomorrow. We need to get to Margaret River. So where do you dive around here?'

Hector looked up from his can. 'Any old hole'll do. Sometimes we drive out west. Aboriginal land. It's a permit job but we know a back way in. There's a big system there. We did a three-day dive last month. Camped underground for two nights and never reached the end. It's sweet, mate, real sweet.' Hector drained his can and, burping like an elephant seal, tossed it out the window. Grabbing a full one, he flipped it open one-handed, took a big swallow and continued. 'Water's as cold as a mother-in-law's kiss, snap your nipples off soon as look at ya. Two nights, mate, underground.' He raised his eyebrows at Goog, so he could appreciate what they had done. 'It's dark as the devil's lunchbox down there. You should come for a look.'

Goog felt the bourbon and cola going thick in his mouth. He thought back to his dream of Castro diving down to meet his fears and then the reality of a great white tearing into him. He thought about the fear that Castro must have felt in his last moments, the terrible knowledge that he was going to die. The shark would have taken him down, drowned him, shaken his body like a dog shakes a rabbit. Goog feared drowning, a stupid fear for a surfer but as real as anything he could touch. Ever since he was a kid he'd believed he would die in the water. He often pictured his death, offshore from some lonely beach, his legrope caught around a fist of stone, body swaying slowly like a rag of kelp and a thin stream of bubbles pearling from his nose. There was no way he would dive under this desert. There was no way he would die this far inland.

The two-up school was not the one in Goog's postcard. This one was four hours' drive down a rough road. There were fifty or so utes parked outside, all of them thick with dust and bristling with hunting lights. There were no tour buses. The school was a ring of corrugated iron fencing with a rough gate facing the road.

Hector was here to meet a Filipino ex-maid turned gold prospector, who was also his dive-buddy and part-time girlfriend. She was tougher than buff steak, missing the tip of her right ear and had a butterfly knife tucked in her left sock. Hector smiled all the time he was talking about her, and he talked a lot on the trip there.

'Goog, this is Jembones.' Hector introduced them over the shouting of the crowd. They had left Aldo asleep in the back of the ute, curled around his eagle corpse.

Jembones ignored Goog. She gave Hector a white-hot stare and prodded him in the soft part of his neck, the hollow where the windpipe is the most vulnerable, making him choke and cough.

'Jooo! I wait por porty minutes for joo. An my name is not Jembones. How many times I tole joo?'

Hector spat a huge oyster onto the red dirt floor. 'Shit, Jem, give us a break will ya. Tryin to kill me or somethin?'

'Joo lucky if I only kill joo. I more than kill joo if joo call me Jembones one more. Understan?'

Hector held up his hand and swallowed, he was having difficulty breathing.

'Come on, joo, buy me a drink.' She got hold of Hector's sleeve and dragged him off towards the bar – two rough-sawn planks on a couple of empty forty-fours.

Goog watched the game for a while and the flat dusty faces of the crowd, their eyes dulled with VB and cheap rum. The spinner called, 'Heademup . . . heademup . . . heademup . . .' Coins glittered as they flew up and spun in the air. Then all eyes down and disappointed as the coins slapped onto the ground – one tail and one head. 'Fuck!' The thrust of another twenty, another fifty. More beer, more rum and coke. The coins up and down. Fists of dirty crumpled notes. 'Heademup . . . heademup . . . heademup . . .' Paypackets ripped open, blowing around. Coins like little fish, little angels, little devils. 'Yesssssss!' A round of beers for everyone. 'Heademup . . .' Heads. 'Yeah! Yeah!' Beer spilling, rum and coke turning the dust dark. Grown men crying, borrowing fifty until payday, blowing it on the next spin. 'Heademup!'

Goog's head began to hurt. He pushed out of the crowd and back through the gate. It was getting dark. The lights came on in the two-up school, a generator thud-thudded nearby. Shutting his eyes, he tried to picture the ocean. It was wrong, this big sun-scarred country, and it scared him. The people were as dry and harsh as the landscape. He needed the softness of salt water, the smell of seaweed and the coolness of wet sand. But even though he screwed his eyes tight on the desert, it still seeped through his eyelids – the hardness of stone, the ridges of corrugated iron, burnt-out cars and black humps of roadkill.

Aldo was still asleep in the back of the ute. Goog grabbed his jacket out of the cab and threw it over him. He got his camera and flash and went back in to find Hector. He was over near the bar, talking to a big man in a sleeveless Yakka shirt. The man was nodding slowly, but as Goog approached, he turned his back and watched the toss of the coins.

Hector said, 'Goog, mate, got a drink? Here, let me buy you one. You must be drier than a nun's nasty. This is Rowdy. Rowdy, turn round and be sociable. This is Goog.'

Rowdy took Goog's hand and gave him the *fucking tough* handshake. Goog got his hand free and clenched and unclenched it to regain circulation.

'Rowdy's a diver, too. Aren'tcha, Rowdy?' Rowdy nodded. 'You can buddy-up with him on the dive, eh, Rowdy?' Rowdy nodded again. 'We'll head out first thing. Rowdy's ute's all packed up and ready. He's got a spare set of tanks that he can lend you.'

This wasn't what Goog needed. He was over adventure, he'd had enough of it to last forever. 'Diving? I didn't say anything about diving. I just wanted to see the two-up school. And what about Aldo? I can't leave him.'

'Goog, no offence but your mate's a bit rattly, if you get my meaning. Got a few roos loose in his top paddock. Not all there. A stubbie short of a six pack. He's not firin on all eight . . .'

Obviously Hector had a hundred different ways to say what was wrong with Aldo, but there was no way Goog was going underground with this bunch of misfits. 'I'm not diving, Hector.' The time for following blindly no matter what was over.

Rowdy looked Goog straight in the eye and said, 'I think this one's a bit of a coward, Hec.'

Goog was shaking, his camera heavy in his hand. He could swing it at Rowdy and knock him out. Instead, he hung it around his neck and said, 'It's got nothing to do with cowardice.'

'It's everything to do with cowardice, boy. You're scared, you've let fear be the master.' Rowdy took a sip from his can.

'There's a difference between bravery and stupidity.'

Rowdy pulled his elbow off the bar and stood up to his full height. 'Did he call us stupid, Hec?'

'I think he did, Rowdy,' said Hector standing beside him. 'Reckon this boy needs some manners teaching to him.'

Goog looked at Hector clenching and unclenching his fist. Then Rowdy's finger stabbed him in the chest and he fell back into the crowd, through the bodies of sweating gamblers and onto the ground. His camera swung up and smacked into his lip. Goog tasted the metallic tang of his own blood.

Down there, among the fag ends and bottletops, the heels of cowboy boots and the desert sand, he saw Rowdy's legs pushing forward towards him. He rolled quickly into an open space. The coins had been tossed and there was a roar from the crowd. Beer slopped over his face as he got to his feet. He elbowed his way through the crowd and up to the ring. The coins were lying on the dirt. Goog knew he needed to create a distraction. Rowdy and Hector would find him here. He leapt forward and grabbed the coins.

There was a slow silence. Big men with tattoos and burnt red faces looked at each other. A lot of money was riding on the last toss. Goog stood up, arced his arm back and threw the coins into the crowd. Everyone looked at him, waiting, wondering what to do next. Then a huge bear of a bloke in stained overalls grabbed him by the shoulder and pulled his fist back to punch him. At the same moment, Goog felt a hand grab his heel and saw the lights of the two-up ring swing into the air. He fell back onto the hard packed soil as above him the air exploded in a volley of fists and forearms. The tension of fifty-hour weeks, dirt, dust and boredom let go in one massive explosion. He tried to get up but a hand stopped him.

'Stay down, mate. Best you keep out of this one.' The man was lying flat on the ground, one hand over his head, the other on Goog's shoulder. 'Something I learnt in the army – the lower you are, the less it hurts. Better we belly-crawl out of here.'

Goog followed the man, keeping his eye on the cracked bare soles of his feet. They got to the gate, stood up and ran towards the cars. People were being thrown against the tin sides of the two-up ring. There was a lot of shouting and the sound of breaking bottles.

'My car's over here.' The man pointed to a rusted old Beetle.

'I need to get someone.' Goog ran over to Hector's ute and shook Aldo awake. He dragged him to the VeeDub before Aldo had a chance to grab his eagle or make a protest.

The man had the car going when they got there and as soon as they were in, he flattened the accelerator to the floor. They fishtailed out onto the road.

'Someone'll radio the coppers and then the shit will really hit the fan.' The Beetle's owner looked at Goog. 'That was some trick you pulled with the coins. What was it all about?'

'Just wanted to see what would happen.' Goog didn't know

if the Beetleman knew Hector or Rowdy but he couldn't take any chances.

'You're a strange one, all right,' Beetleman said. 'And what's with your mate in the back? He's a bit on the nose.'

That was putting it mildly; Aldo stank like a three-day-old carcass.

Goog said, 'Something bad happened to him.'

'No shit,' said Beetleman. 'What was it exactly?'

Goog looked at Aldo's dark form. 'We don't like to talk about it.'

Beetleman stared into the dark ahead and said, 'I can respect that.'

Aldo stirred. 'Where's my eagle, Goog?' he asked.

'It's gone,' replied Goog. 'Flew on home. Missed its friends and family and its old town.'

'That's good, Goog,' said Aldo. 'That's all I wanted.'

The sky was cold and clear, full of bright stars. A satellite struck out from the north and Goog watched until it set over the horizon. He imagined the silence of space, the distance and the darkness. From up there this would all seem so insignificant. From up there they wouldn't even register as specks.

They had been driving for hours with Aldo's snores and the VeeDub's throaty growl filling their silence.

Beetleman looked into the beam of his headlights. The light from the rising sun slipped across his profile, highlighting his big curved nose and his white bandana. His white hair hung around his head like mist. 'This desert is too big sometimes. Swallow you whole if you let it. What you blokes wanna come here for?'

Goog touched his lip and rubbed a thin smear of blood between his fingers. 'My dad came here when I was ten. He was a miner. Before that, he was an odd-job man in Torquay. And before that, Vietnam . . .' The words trailed away.

'Yeah, me as well.'

'Maybe you knew him – Bill Leary?'

'Lotta bodies in Nam. I didn't get to meet all of them. I guess you miss him, eh?'

'Feels like I hardly knew him. But sometimes I think of him and they're good thoughts, mostly.'

They pulled off the dirt and down a side road. 'I gotta get some juice for this old bird.' Beetleman patted the steering wheel. 'There's some friends down here that'll fix us up.'

Coming up to the camp, Goog could see a rusty pile of dead cars and a snarl of ring-tailed dogs. A circle of tin humpies sheltered sleeping bodies. They pulled up beside an aluminium shed with towers of forty-four-gallon drums stacked against one wall. Beetleman stopped the car, got out and slapped the side of the shed with his hand.

'Y'wake in there?' He waited a few seconds, looked around camp, slapped again. 'Wake up, y'dozy bugger.'

An Aboriginal man came to the door, blinking the morning cloud from his eyes. He had a thick wool blanket over his shoulders and was shivering in the chill. 'Whatcha want this time of the mornin?' he asked. 'Can't a fella get a lie-in?'

'Need a bit of go-juice, Brillo. Been out at the two-up, getting rich.'

Brillo snorted at this. 'Right.' He nodded at the VeeDub. 'Who's the hitchers?'

'Just a coupla kids from out east. Ran into a bit of strife at the ring.'

'Youse got time for a coffee?' Brillo asked.

'Aw, mate, I gotta get back to town. Better just get the juice and get back on the road.'

'Help yourself. You know where it is.'

Brillo went back inside and Goog followed Beetleman over to the forty-fours. 'Give that handle a bit of a turn,' said Beetleman as he poked the hose into the car.

While Goog pumped petrol, Beetleman talked.

'So, your dad ever tell you about the war?'

Goog shook his head.

'It wasn't easy being over there, seeing all those things and then coming home. Some experiences change you forever. Some of them make you stronger but some weaken you in ways people can't see. How long since you saw him?'

Goog looked into Beetleman's dark pupils. 'Eight years.'

'He's probably moved on long ago. I've never even heard of him and I know just about everyone around here.' Beetleman paused, rattled his fingers on the roof of the car. 'Thought about what you're gonna do when you find him?'

Goog stopped pumping. If he came face to face with him, would he know what to say? Would he have the courage to speak his mind, to dig up what he had buried for eight years? He searched Beetleman for clues – his ragged work shirt, his oily moleskins, the battered leather of his face. Beetleman stared back at him.

'I'm going to ask him why he left,' Goog said, finally.

The day was beginning to unfold, light wandering into the ragged camp, the tangles of rusted metal and broken-armed trees. Long shadows were fingering the cracked earth.

The man took the pump handle from Goog and continued filling the Beetle. 'I'm sure he won't be able to tell you why he left.'

Brillo's head appeared around the side of the shed. 'Come in for a coffee. Can't sleep with you clatterin round out here.'

Goog looked at Aldo snoring quietly in the car.

'Leave him to sleep,' said Beetleman. 'Looks like he could use it.'

They went into the shed. It was dark and smelt of woodsmoke. There was an open fire in the centre of the room and a hole in the roof that let most of the smoke escape. As Goog's eyes grew used to the dark, he saw photos Blu-Tacked to the wall. Closer up, he could see they were black-and-whites – landscapes and macros of plants and rocks. They were full of texture, jammed with the patterns of the desert. They reminded Goog of the dot paintings he had seen in art books and on gallery walls, paintings by desert people. In the fire's orange glow they took on a mystic quality.

'Like my pics?' Brillo had come up behind him with a cup of coffee.

'They're great, man,' Goog said, taking the hot mug from him.

'I love it, takin them. They're a way of unlockin stuff inside you. Makin how you feel about a place or a person come alive on paper. Some people reckon it's not art but they're full of shit.'

Goog said, 'I used to take photos. They were okay, but I think I got a bit caught up with being behind the lens, didn't allow myself to see things for real.'

'Thassa trap, for sure. Maybe you gotta use the camera to show yourself to the world instead of just hidin behind it.'

There was a scream from outside and a chorus of barks from the camp dogs. Goog ran for the door and opened it to see Aldo crouched in the back seat of the Beetle. On and around the car was a ragged assortment of kids. They were wild and happy, all bright smiles and hair scoured blond by the desert sun. One of them, a boy of seven or eight in a green Staminade tracksuit and rubber boots, had conquered the curving roof. A couple of young girls were using the windscreen as a slide, another had tied her skipping rope to the door handle and was chanting as two friends jumped. Aldo had woken to a hallucination – one where his world had been overrun by Aboriginal kids.

Brillo just laughed. 'What's with your mate? This is the kids' patch, they gotta right to play here.'

'We should go,' said Beetleman, looking at Aldo's cowering form. 'Thanks for the coffee, Brillo. What do I owe you for the juice?'

'Don't worry bout it. But if you're goin to town, could you post somethin for me?' Brillo went inside and came back with a brown envelope. 'Just some pics for a gallery back east.' He shrugged as if it meant nothing to him. 'Gotta pay for chemicals and paper somehow.'

Goog forgot about Aldo for a moment. 'Your work's on show?'

'Brillo's famous back east. Aren'tcha?' Beetleman said. 'Trendies like to hang a piece of the rugged desert on them smooth plaster walls.'

'That's enough bout me. But you should keep on takin them pics, mate. People'll pay to see the world through your eyes.'

As they drove slowly out of the camp, followed by the kids and dogs, Goog picked up his camera. *If only I knew what I wanted*, he thought, *life would be so simple*. He leant out the window and shot a couple of frames of the kid in the Staminade tracksuit, the wild nest of his hair blown through with desert sand and his eyes bright with the promise of childhood.

As they worked along the rutted road towards the highway, Aldo asked, 'Where we going, Goog?'

'We're heading back,' Goog answered.

'Back home?' The eagerness in Aldo's voice made Goog sink inside.

'To Kalgoorlie, Aldo. We're going to Margaret River, remember?'

'What are we doing in Kalgoorlie, Goog?'

'I dunno, Aldo,' said Goog. 'But whatever it was, it's finished now.'

12

FLAT CHAT

It was time for some night driving and fuck the kangaroos. Beetleman's car had given up the ghost twenty k's from the Aboriginal camp and they had spent the rest of the day fixing it. Now Goog knew why his dad called the old VeeDub *Hitler's revenge*. They gurgled back into Kalgoorlie just as night came sneaking up the highway. Beetleman dropped them back at the Kingswood and wished them luck.

Goog and Aldo stood listening to the thud of a Cold Chisel cover band warming up inside the pub. Gangs of jacked-up utes crawled past, their passengers spraying foam and foul language onto the street.

Aldo began to shiver. He was wearing only his filthy T-shirt and the night had gone cold.

'Let's go,' Goog said and slipped the key into the lock. He pulled on the handle but discovered he'd locked the door instead of opening it. Then he noticed that the button on Aldo's door was up and the tailgate window was wide open. Goog was sure he had locked up before they left. He turned the key again, opened the door and checked to see if anything was missing.

The dash was covered in dead blowflies. As the door light

came on, a few survivors bumbled over the carpet to suck on the remains of the eagle blood. Goog crunched a hundred dry corpses as he got in. Everything looked like it was there.

He cranked the Kingswood over. It wheezed unhappily and barked up a clot of oil and smoke. He turned the key again and the starter motor jammed open with a noise like a key on new duco. The battery was dropping amps. Its terminals were covered in white bloom and it was cold and tired. Goog rested his forehead on the steering wheel and tried the motor again. The cam rotated slowly, the piston arms pushing through burnt oil. The slow winding down of the car's mechanics dried Goog's throat and made him feel sick. They couldn't stay here. What would he do if Hector or Rowdy turned up? Or Jem with her butterfly knife and her scary attitude?

The handle on the bonnet release was a loop of coathanger wire. It cut into Goog's fingers as he pulled it. He walked to the front of the car, undid the safety catch and opened the bonnet. It was dark inside, too dark to make out anything important.

'Aldo, throw me the torch out of the glovebox.' Goog waited, staring into the darkness, while he pictured Aldo undoing the ockie strap and fumbling for the torch.

'Aldo! The torch! I need it, mate.'

Utes were beginning to slow down. A beer bottle was smashed into the gutter. It would be a good idea to be somewhere else, and quickly.

'Aldo!'

When Goog walked around to the passenger-side door, Aldo was asleep again. Reaching in the half-open window, he grubbed around in the glovebox for the torch. When he returned to the front of the car, a man with a flask of whisky was peering in at the engine.

'Vot's the problem vit de car?' he said as he swayed gently in an imaginary breeze. He was small, smaller than Goog, and wore a pair of torn blue overalls with a Dutch flag sewn on the front pocket. His hair was as white as river sand and his nose ended in a bubble that dimpled in the middle like a peach.

'Dunno, mate,' Goog said in gruff Aussie, designed to inspire mateship and get rid of weirdos.

The man pointed the neck of his bottle at a doorway. 'I hear her from over dere and she sound like she bloody not firing. Sokay, I give you a hand.'

He grabbed the torch from Goog and gripped it between his teeth. Reaching into the engine bay, he flipped open the distributor cap and chuckled quietly. Then, taking the torch into his hand again, he directed the beam into the distributor. 'See here,' he said, pointing into the beam. 'More like vot you *don't* bloody see, eh?' And he chuckled again, the little points of his shoulders jumping up and down.

Goog didn't get the joke but he didn't want to appear stupid either. 'Yeah, it's um, not that great is it?'

'You're not bloody choking, mate.' It took Goog a moment to realise he meant 'joking'. 'You bloody got no bloody rotor button, mate. Maybe your bloody mate took it out for a choke.'

Goog doubted if his mate was in much of a state for a *choke*. Then it dawned on him who might have done it. Maybe not as a joke – but Rowdy or Hector would have been in town way before them. Goog shrugged off the idea. Why would they bother?

'You haven't got a spare, have you, mate? I'll pay you.'

The man's shoulders jumped around and his sharp little Adam's apple bobbed like a cork. 'Heh heh heh heh heh heh. Wery bloody funny, mate.' He took a swig from his hip flask:

Johnny Walker Red, Goog noticed, the man was no dero. When he reached out and put a hand on Goog's shoulder, his breath was sour with whisky and garlic. He couldn't stop laughing. 'Heh heh heh heh heh. Spare? Heh heh heh heh heh.'

Goog was sickened by the drunk. His shoulders were snowed with dandruff. Goog could see through his thin hair to his red flaking scalp.

'Heh heh heh heh.'

Goog shrugged off the arm and grabbed his torch. The man kept on laughing, harder if anything, stopping only to empty a measure of Johnny Walker down his throat. Goog walked away from Mr Chuckles and climbed back inside the car.

'Heh heh heh heh heh heh heh.' Mr Chuckles pointed at Goog with his bottle, toasted him through the windscreen and swallowed a gulp. 'Heh heh heh heh,' he spluttered, whisky spilling from his mouth. Then he stuffed the flask into his overalls and swayed his way down the street, turning into a skimpy bar that promised *Half Prise Beer Thusday*.

Goog leant his head back on the seat. He closed his eyes for a moment. Just a moment.

Goog remembered basic mechanics with Dad. Saturday afternoons, bent beneath the bonnet of their old Valiant, with Mum bringing them cups of sweet tea and Iced Vo Vos on a dinner plate.

'The ignition system has an alternator to generate the current, a coil to boost it, a distributor to distribute the spark and spark plugs to fire the fuel-air mix.' Dad's hair was pulled back with one of Mum's hair ties and he had a streak of grease down his left cheek. It was always his left cheek.

Mum came out with the biscuits and tea and ruffled Goog's hair. He hated that.

Dad kissed Mum, leaving grease on her chin, then continued. 'Here's the distributor.' He tapped the side of it with a screwdriver then flipped it open and pulled out a piece of red plastic with a brass strip. 'And this is the rotor button. Without it, the car doesn't go. This fella dishes out the spark to the high-tension leads.' He pointed with his screwdriver to a tangle of blue wires. 'It's an important little number. Very important.' And he placed the piece gently in Goog's palm.

A knock on the window woke Goog. The face scared the shit out of him, but even more shocking were the fingers. Long praying-mantis fingers, stick-fingers. They were knocking the window with a piece of red plastic.

It had been nearly a week since Goog had last seen Jasper and he hadn't missed him at all. He wound the window down half a turn and said, 'What are you doing here? What do you want from us?'

Jasper waved the rotor button at Goog. 'One question at a time, Goog. I'll take the last one first – another lift would be nice.'

'Piss off. Just piss off, okay.' Goog was shaking badly as he rolled the window back up. Aldo woke up and, crouching on the floor, began to whine like a dog.

Pressing his face up against the glass, Jasper said, 'You may as well bed down with the coyote, boys. He's going to get you anyway.' He widened his mouth against the window, until they could see the black holes in his teeth.

Goog had no idea what Jasper was on about. Had no idea

what he was *on* and wanted no part of him. It was the only thing that Aldo and Goog had agreed on, before Aldo left for la-la land. Jasper was trouble.

'Open up, boys. I have the medicine for what ails you.'

Jasper tapped the window with the rotor button. Aldo began to wail. Goog turned on the radio and cranked it up until it became the only noise he could hear. The volume was incredible. Jasper looked around him. Drunks were beginning to stumble out of the pubs and utes were slowing to a crawl to see what the trouble was. The cat's song of a police siren got louder as it came closer. Jasper sneered at Goog, gave the window a lick and placed the rotor button on the roof. Goog watched him take his pole-vaulter's stride down the main street and out of sight. The siren turned away and died.

They stayed in the car for a very long time, with the radio belting out country tunes to keep the night-horrors away. Aldo fell asleep, his head on the seat and his body cramped beneath the glovebox. Goog turned the radio down and, after a while, off completely. He sat in silence watching two dogs fight it out on the pavement. Then, plucking courage from somewhere new, he opened the door and stepped out into the cold street.

It was quiet outside. Everyone was sleeping off yesterday's pay. The pubs were shut for the few hours until early swill. In the next street a car laid down some rubber and someone shouted. The rotor button was still on the roof. Goog clicked open the bonnet and shone the torch at the distributor. Mr Chuckles had left the cap off, so Goog clipped the button down on the shaft and replaced the cap. He got back inside the car and turned the motor over. Click . . . click . . . nothing. The battery was completely dead. He would have to roll-start and he would be doing it alone.

There was just enough slope to get the Beast rolling. Goog pushed hard on the door and the car began to move forward. He dropped his shoulder and allowed his legs to stretch out behind him, leaning his full weight against the window. It had to be enough speed. He jumped in and found second gear. When he dropped the clutch, the car stuttered but didn't fire. Quickly pulling it out of gear, he jumped out and shouldered the door again. On the second attempt the engine fired and Goog quickly pushed the clutch in and revved hard.

On the outskirts of town, they stopped at a servo and fuelled up. Goog picked up a map of the south-west. It was cheap and badly made and there would be place names missing for sure, but it was all that was available. Leaning against the news-stand, he unfolded it.

Over to the far west, his fingers found the pignose, bounded at each nostril by Cape Leeuwin and Cape Naturaliste. In the middle of the nose, where the ring would be, was Margaret River. In between, there was a nest of lines that Goog would have to drive through. He could head out west on the highway as far as Merredin and then take the thin red road to Corrigin. After Corrigin the red road petered out into thin double-lined roads, identified only as *other roads*. Goog figured that if he could work his way through these, he would hit Narrogin and a road that headed west again.

Merredin, Corrigin, Narrogin, Merredin, Corrigin, Narrogin, Merredin, Corrigin . . .

The road was alive with shadows and red eyes. Goog's own eyes were stretched wide in an attempt to stay awake. His stomach was rumbling for food but even if there was a shop open, there was no way he was going to stop. He would die of hunger first.

The road map lay unfolded on his lap – Geraldton spilling over his knees, Perth drenched in the darkness between him and Aldo. Goog didn't even know if this road was on the map. It was small. Definitely an *other road*.

They had hit Merredin sometime after two in the morning, fuelled up and headed south. Corrigin should have shown itself over an hour ago. Goog could see the moon running along outside his window, low on the horizon. That had to be west. East was to his left and they must be (they had to be) going south. Every now and then the road would end in a T-intersection, where he would always take the right fork, the one that led to the moon. West. West and south. They would get there like this, Goog was sure.

Up ahead, he could see the blinking of a roadhouse sign. He was dying to take a leak and it would be good to do it somewhere safe. The darkness outside was no longer the harmless creature it used to be.

The Sandy Nook Roadhouse = Petrol and Meat Pi's was set back from the road. Its sign was full of shotgun pellets and the neon strip around it shivered in the black air. Goog crunched the Kingswood onto the gravel forecourt and stalled the motor. He got out of the car, trying not to wake Aldo.

The roadhouse itself was in darkness. Rather than piss out in the open, Goog walked around the side, where a stand of salmon gums whispered softly. He walked among them, running his hand over smooth bark, until he was sheltered from the road.

A dog barked and threw itself against a cyclone-wire fence. A light went on and someone yelled out, 'Shut the fuck up,

Buster!' The dog knew that his owner had gone to some effort to turn the light on. The dog knew the next step in the program and *shut the fuck up*.

Goog let out a stream on the nearest tree trunk. It steamed and ran in a puddle to his feet. He stepped back, keeping his piss arced onto the trunk, and looked up through the branches and hissing leaves to the cloud of the milky way. A star burnt in the gaps of the canopy and a bat swooped on a moth. Then Goog heard the drone of a motorbike winding up the road. He couldn't see any light but as it came closer he heard the rattle of its exhaust and a pop as it misfired. Then the engine noise stopped and there were only the sounds of night – the hissing leaves and the strangled croak of a frog in the water tank. He finished, then turned and picked his way between the trees and back to the car. There was no motorbike around. Maybe he had just imagined it. God, he needed sleep.

The Kingswood started first pop. They were a kilometre down the road before the roadhouse owner gave in to insomnia and went down to beat her dog.

Goog clicked his neck from side to side and wriggled some comfort out of the seat. Trees appeared by the road, dark figures with stars worrying their crowns like fireflies. There were no trucks or cars and Aldo was asleep. He was alone, with the steady growl of the Kingswood's diff. Alone, with the pinging of gravel under the wheel arches.

And then he felt a hand on his shoulder. At first it seemed like a hallucination – as if the lack of sleep and the stress of the past week had finally unhinged his mind. But the hand seemed solid. The fingers felt real as they wrapped over his collarbone.

The moon was ducking behind the tailgate, darting between trees. In the flashes of light, Goog caught a glimpse of the hand in the rear-view mirror. The nails were long, raw and bloody at the quick. The fingers were thin, knuckles standing out like knotted ropes, and long. Very long.

Goog's throat was so tight that he could only manage a raspy cough. Aldo's head moved on the seat beside him.

'The coyote catches up. How have you been since our evening in the desert?' Jasper leant over Goog's shoulder, his bald head waxy in the moonlight. His breath smelled of spearmint, as he whispered into Goog's ear, 'I know about Castro.'

Goog spun the wheel over, slamming Jasper's head into the window. Aldo slid into Goog's lap and woke with a scream. He was trapped under Goog's arms. As he fought to free himself from the nightmare, Goog struggled to control the car. Finally he managed to release Aldo and slide the car onto the verge.

The car's stuffed valves clicked noisily. Goog's heart bounced in his chest. He watched as Jasper's fingernail carefully scooped a bead of blood from near his temple.

'Why can't you leave us alone?' Goog said, but he knew the answer. Jasper was after the Zip. Goog looked at his yellow skull and his cold blue eyes. There was no way he was going to give Jasper the disk, Castro wouldn't have wanted that. 'Just piss off and leave us,' he said.

'Is that any way to speak to an old friend?'

'You're not our friend. You did something to Castro, didn't you?' It felt good, it felt right to lay the final blame with Jasper.

'We made a deal, Castro and I. I honoured my part but Castro let me down. Now I'm back to collect.'

'Castro?' asked Aldo. He looked into the back seat at Jasper, his eyes ringed heavily with black, a faint crust of eagle blood still on his cheek.

Jasper pressed his palms together as if he was about to pray.

'How the mighty have fallen.' He brought his fingertips to his lips.

'Leave him alone! This is between you and me. What did you do to Castro that night?' Goog was almost in the back seat with Jasper. Diamonds of his spit flew onto the man's cheeks.

'I didn't do anything, I was just the catalyst for change.'

Goog clenched his fists at this bullshit. He wanted to punch it back down Jasper's fucking throat.

Aldo was back on the floor, his knuckles pressed deep into his eye sockets.

Goog yelled, 'Get out. Get out of my fucking car!'

'Correct me if I'm wrong, but isn't it his car?' Jasper snaked a finger at Aldo. 'And it looks like he's in need of some help.'

'Not from you. This is all your fault!' Goog flat-palmed the top of the seat and Aldo jumped.

Jasper said, 'You can blame the coyote or you can run with him.'

Goog said, 'What the fuck is all this coyote crap? You make it sound like a "Roadrunner" cartoon. These are people's lives you're messing with! What makes you think we have what you want, anyway?'

'Oh, you have it, all right, and I'm sticking around until I get it. I have things to trade. I can help you with Aldo. I can tell you things about Castro, things you never knew.'

Goog jumped out of the car and wrenched the back door open. 'Get out! Now!' he shouted.

Jasper was wearing a day-glo road-worker's vest. Goog grabbed it and pulled him out onto the road. He lay there and looked up at him.

'You need me, Goog. Aldo needs me. It's time to work on those tough decisions.'

Goog corked him in the thigh with the tip of his runner, so hard that Jasper balled-up in pain. He got back in the car and slammed the door. *Fuck him,* he thought, *I can do this alone. Nothing he can tell me about Castro will help me now.* But the longer he sat there, breathing mist onto the window and listening to Aldo's sobs, the less sure he was.

'I Blame Me.' Aldo pointed at the registration plate of the car in front. 'It's my fault that Castro died.'

Jasper had suggested the game as soon as dawn broke and cars reappeared on the road. *Automotive Therapy* he called it. Only Victorian plates – there were few of them on this road and it gave them time to think. They had to start with the first three letters of the rego, make a phrase and then talk about it. The others could respond if they wanted or let it pass on to the next person.

The car in front was a Mazda wagon, rego number IBM 963. Jasper had given Aldo the first shot.

'Castro left you because he had to. It was his time to go. There is no blame,' Jasper said.

Aldo's brow furrowed like high-pressure lines on a swell map. 'I don't feel the same any more. I don't know who I am.'

Jasper left this alone. It sat in the air like fog.

'Your turn, Goog,' he said, looking in the rear-view.

'Pass,' Goog said, and drummed the dash with his fingers to drown the silence.

It was a while before the next Victorian car came along. Goog had almost forgotten about the game when Jasper said, 'We Are Chesspieces . . . in the hands of gods.'

'No!' said Aldo. 'No! You can't have all those letters.'

Jasper patted him on the shoulder. 'Okay, then, just We Are Chesspieces. The jury should disregard the last part of the statement.'

Goog replied, 'Wankers Appear Clever,' and met Jasper's eyes in the mirror.

It took a moment for Jasper to reply. 'Wasting Advice is Close-minded.' The corners of his lips turned up and he darted his bony forefinger at Goog's reflection.

'Why Are Creeps like you allowed in this world?'

'No!' Aldo dropped in again, 'We gotta follow the rules. Go again, Goog.'

'We Allowed Castro.' Goog wiped at a tear that had appeared, unwanted, in the corner of his eye.

'That doesn't make any sense —' Aldo began but Jasper's hand came down on his shoulder and silenced him.

'We allowed Castro to be our hope. We allowed him to be our dreamer. We allowed him to take all the risks. We allowed him to die.' Goog could barely see the road any more through his tears.

'We allowed him to be our mate,' Aldo said.

'We allowed him to move on,' said Jasper.

Goog screamed, 'You don't have a right! You don't have a right to him. He was our mate.'

'He was everyone's mate, Goog. Sooner or later he had to do something for himself.'

'Are you saying that he killed himself? It was a shark attack, for fuck's sake!'

'I'm saying that he chose his own path.'

They were quiet for a long time.

Then Aldo said, 'She'll Be Right,' and pointed back at a red Corolla that had just passed them heading east. Goog squinted in the mirror but he couldn't make out the rego number. They were moving away from each other at two hundred kilometres an hour.

They couldn't find anything on their map. Jasper had it in the back and every time they snuck up on a pub or general store, he ran his fingers over lines and into folds but failed to uncover the name.

'I thought you were some great traveller. You should know where we are.' Goog didn't understand how Jasper had tricked his way back into their lives. It made him mad. It made him want to punish the bastard. 'You're just a sad old man. A has-been, a wannabe bloodsucking leech.'

Jasper sat through it all, his fingers splayed out over the map like huntsman spiders.

Goog continued, 'So desperate you turn to the Brotherhood of —' He stopped himself but not soon enough. In the back seat Jasper was folding up the map and smiling.

'Ah yes, the Brotherhood of Aryan ResponsiBility. I was wondering when that would come up,' said Jasper, 'We had a business arrangement, which our sleepy friend ballsed up. And then your hero Castro stole a computer disk that I was sent to retrieve. The Brotherhood had some police hassles, had their computer impounded. To get their website up and running, the Brotherhood needs that disk. Do you know anything of its whereabouts?'

Goog imagined he could hear the Zip rattling against the door panel.

'I haven't got a clue what you're talking about.' No way he was giving it up, no way. It was the only card he held in a game that Jasper played only too well.

'Well, then, maybe Aldo does.' Jasper went to shake him but Goog pushed his hand away.

'Look at him. He can hardly remember his own name. And do you think he would do anything that would harm his bloody Brotherhood? Do you?' It was crazy but he still felt the need to protect Aldo. And there was always the danger he would remember their conversation about the disk in Norseman.

Opening the map again, Jasper said, 'Two things about me, Goog: I'm patient, and I always get what I want. One of you knows and one of you is going to tell me. It looks like Aldo will be the easiest nut to crack.'

The fuel needle was down near empty; they would need to stop soon. Up ahead there was a sign. Goog leant forward and read it, between the beetles and moths that smattered the windscreen: *Porriwong pop. 18—* Someone had removed the bottom right-hand corner with their car.

Porriwong had a servo, an old one, with driveway service and refillable glass oil bottles. They ran over the pressure hose, triggering a bell that triggered a man who came out wiping his chapped pink hands on a washcloth.

'What c'n I do you for?' he said as he tunnelled at his ear with the cloth.

'Fill her up with leaded,' said Goog, getting out of the car.

'No worries,' said the man, unhooking the pump.

Goog leant on the bonnet and watched the man fill the car. 'Nice morning,' he said.

'Rain before the day's through, if I'm not mistaken.' The man crouched down and stuffed the washcloth into the breast pocket of his overalls.

Goog asked, 'Where are we anyway?' They needed directions as badly as they needed fuel. The sign had said Porriwong but where the hell was Porriwong?

The man looked up at Goog. 'Bout hundred and fifty clicks north of Mount Barker. Big city, Mount Barker. Never bin there mesel.' Some petrol burped back to the nozzle, so the man pulled it out a fraction and eased in another dollar. He replaced the cap and wiped around it with the washcloth.

Jasper leant out of the window with the map. 'Did you say Mount Barker? I see where we are now.'

Goog walked over to Jasper and looked down at the tip of his finger. It was only a hand's width from the bottom of the country. They had come too far south. Way too far south.

'Here's the new plan,' said Jasper over breakfast. They were still in Porriwong, eating sausage rolls on the bonnet of the Kingswood. 'We drive to Mount Barker and then strike out on the Muirs Highway towards Manjimup. Here.' He brushed some sausage meat off a road about twenty k's outside Manjimup. 'We take this road to Pemberton. Then we shoot out west until we meet the Bussell Highway. After that, it's north to Margaret River. Shouldn't take us more than five hours.'

'Who died and made you king?' said Goog. There was no way Jasper should be telling them what to do. This wasn't his trip. It wasn't his car. If only Goog could get the info on Castro without giving up the Zip, then they could just drive away and leave Jasper behind.

Jasper sighed, picked a flake of pastry from the corner of his mouth. 'Goog, someone has to make the decisions here.

If you're driving, I'll navigate. It just makes sense.'

Goog wasn't happy with the situation but he was too tired to argue. 'Navigator or not, you still have to ride in the back.' At least he could keep Jasper away from Aldo.

'Sure, I'll ride in the back. Wouldn't want to come between you and your friend.'

No, you've already done that once, thought Goog.

13

THE GLOUCESTER TREE

At the milk bar in Pemberton, they bought hot chicken rolls
and ate them in the shop, while they watched the owner slicing
up tomatoes for the sandwich bar. He was shredding a Redhead
between tombstone teeth. 'You gotta check out the Gloucester
Tree,' he said and rolled the match neatly over to the other corner of his mouth. 'Big bloody tree that and no mistake. Sixty
metres, if it's an inch. Fella named Jack Watson climbed it in
forty-seven. Took the poor bastard six hours. They were a
tougher mob then, the forestry workers. Not the tree-hugger
nancy-boys they are now. It was a fire lookout up till seventy-
four.'

He spat the match onto the floor and slipped the tomatoes
into a stainless-steel container.

Jasper was leaning on the counter and dropping chicken
onto the licorice display. He finished his roll, scrunched up the
bag and tossed it in the bin.

'Let's go,' he said and walked out the door, without even
looking back at their match-chewing tourist guide.

Back at the Kingswood, Goog and Aldo found Jasper in the

driver's seat. Goog opened the driver's door and said, 'You're in the back, Jasper. We agreed.'

'Oh, Goog. Things change. Now I'm in the front. Aldo and I have a lot to talk about. Don't we, Aldo?'

Aldo nodded and, climbing in beside Jasper, smiled happily out the window.

Goog slammed the front door. 'You're pushing it too far, Jasper.' But he climbed in the back, with his bruised ego and Jasper's improbable Castro knowledge competing for space inside his aching head.

Jasper started the car and swung out wide into the road; as he corrected they were nearly taken out by a logging truck. Goog reached forward and grabbed the map from beside Aldo. Unfolding it on the back seat, he found Kalgoorlie. He ran his finger south to Mount Barker and then out west to the pig-snout cape and Margaret River. Fifty more k's and they would have hit Albany and the ocean.

Goog closed his eyes and imagined a steep, sloping beach, a solid wedge of a wave opening into an Indian Ocean barrel. Of course, it was still the Southern Ocean at Albany but it was only a matter of a couple of hundred kilometres before the continent veered north and the Indian Ocean began for real. They should have gone that way, next to the ocean. Jasper had no feeling for the sea and had decided for all of them. Goog hated that but he needed to keep Jasper sweet. The bastard held almost all the cards.

On the map, outside Pemberton, was Lake Jasper, a small, blue diamond caught between the highway and the coast. If Goog told Jasper about the lake, he would definitely want to stop. The man had an ego the size of a small country. It already felt as if they would never get to Margaret River, as if someone kept moving it just as they were going to make it. So Goog crossed out Lake Jasper with a ballpoint and wrote above it: *Lake Castro.*

The Karri forest towered above them, raining down small nuts and leaves. A dampness in the air furred up wool jumpers and clung softly to beards. There were a lot of beards and jumpers here.

Goog felt uneasy in his nylon rainjacket, with his razor-clean face. Even Aldo looked more at home with his sprouting beard and half-crop of hair. Jasper was still in his orange road-worker's vest.

They clumped over the wooden boardwalk and stood under the Gloucester Tree. It was stupidly tall. Impossibly tall. Goog's throat was exposed to the patches of grey sky above, the back of his head folded onto the nape of his neck. His camera couldn't find the top of the tree. He hadn't held it since the night at the two-up school and it felt like a lump of lead in his hand. There was grit in the focus ring and sticky beer stains on the strap. If he'd brought a wide-angle, twenty millimetre or so, then maybe he could get it all in. But even then, the crown would have been a pinprick and the lookout hut a black smudge on the lens. He took a token shot of the crown and a close-up of bark. It was the best he could do.

He sat with his back against the broad trunk and tried to calm himself. Just when Margaret River had seemed within their grasp, Jasper had made this stop. He hadn't even asked them. Aldo was happy enough, though. There he was, following Jasper over to the information sign like a lost sheep. At least it took the pressure off Goog. He knew Aldo was searching for a new leader since Castro had disappeared.

Jasper came up, blowing into his hands and looking up at the tree. 'Let's go.'

'We're not leaving already? This stop was your idea and we only just got here.'

Here was Jasper making all the rules again. The only thing that kept him in top position was the knowledge he had on Castro. Goog could make a straight trade for the disk here and now and get Jasper out of their lives forever. What would Castro have done?

Aldo edged nervously from one foot to another. He was wearing his stupid grin and a Geelong Cats beanie pulled down too low. 'We're going to climb the tree, Goog.'

Goog looked at the ladder spiralling up the tree and the bearded-jumpers solemnly climbing, their hands like bird talons on the rungs, their boots dropping clods of mud down to the ground.

'I'll wait here,' he said.

The ground was damp and Goog felt cold. He wanted to climb back into the car and go to sleep.

'Come up with us, Goog.' Jasper's voice was quiet and even.

'Yeah, Goog,' said Aldo. 'I won't even try and shake you off this time. It won't be like that day at *Ladders*.'

Aldo was a stupid fuck before, but now he was a *retarded* stupid fuck. Goog loathed him for that and loathed Jasper for controlling everything.

'Fuck you. Both of you! I'm not going up.'

'Face your fears, Goog. Don't be a prisoner of your past.' Jasper was leaning on the tree above him, looking down into his face.

'Fuck you, Mr Freud. I don't give a shit what you think. You may have Aldo fooled but he's so desperate that he'd cling to anything right now.'

Aldo stepped forward, his big fists bunched by his side. Goog's words had pierced Aldo's shield, found the part of his mind where the old Aldo lay. It gave Goog hope that maybe things would return to normal. But Jasper placed a long tapered hand on Aldo's chest and stopped him.

From half a metre away Aldo kicked a clod of dirt and leaves onto Goog. A spark of the old Aldo flared in his eyes and he said, 'You're a wanker, Goog. Always were. It's always me me me. That's what Marcella said and it's true.'

Goog tried to jump to his feet but the ground was slippery and he fell. His body glanced off the tree and he landed on his back in the mud and leaf litter. He wanted to hurt Aldo. Hurt him for what he did to Castro. For what he had done with Marcella. For all the shit he had given him since primary school. Goog had always been too afraid of Aldo; there had always seemed to be a better moment for revenge.

He wanted to get up but Aldo dropped onto him before he could make it. Aldo pushed Goog down and pummelled his chest with his fists. 'You shit me, Goog,' he shouted. His eyes were crazy wide and flecks of spit exploded from his mouth like shattered glass. 'You've always had everything – Castro, Marcella, all the mates you could poke a stick at. You fucken shit me.'

The bearded-jumpers were shouting, 'Hey! hey! hey!' and shaking their dreadlocks at them. Jasper was leaning against the tree, smiling like a tolerant parent. Goog grabbed Aldo's wrists, which stopped the punches, but then he began to head-butt him in the chest. Goog threw his arms around Aldo and held him. Aldo struggled for a moment but then his body went slack and he began to sob.

'You shit me, Goog,' he said, as he buried his face in Goog's jacket and cried.

But Goog knew it wasn't about him. It never had been. 'It's okay, Aldo. It's going to be okay.'

'I miss Castro so much.'

'I do too, Aldo. But he's gone and we have to learn to live without him.'

'I can't,' said Aldo, 'I need someone.'

'Well, it can't be me, Aldo,' said Goog.

Aldo pulled back and looked at him, his eyes red, rimmed with black. There was hurt in there and something Goog recognised as the old anger. But then Aldo blinked and it was gone, replaced with the dumb childishness of the past few days.

The park ranger strode up in his big Blundstones. Goog and Aldo glanced up at his wide-brim Akubra and long sideburns. He stared at them, covered in mud and Aldo's tears.

'What's going on here?' the ranger asked.

'We were just mucking around. Eh, Aldo?'

'Yeah, that's all. Just muckin around.'

The bearded-jumpers clambered back down and offered themselves as witnesses. The ranger said thanks, but there would be no trial. After he had lurched off in his four-wheel drive, Jasper appeared out of the forest and made his way back to the Gloucester Tree.

'Quite a show, chaps,' he said.

Goog brushed mud off his jeans. 'Where'd you get to?'

'I was nearby.' A floating leaf dropped between Goog and Jasper. 'Now that the preliminaries are over, shall we climb?'

Aldo nodded and put his hand on the first peg. Goog got hold of the back of Aldo's jumper and said, 'Wait, Aldo! What's going on here? This is crazy, mate. This guy's nothing to us.'

'I want to, Goog. I want to go up there for Castro. Jasper said it would help.'

He shrugged Goog's hand off and began to climb. Jasper pushed past Goog and started up the ladder too. Now there was only Goog on the ground. The bearded-jumpers had reached the platform and were cooeeing across the treetops. Aldo and Jasper became black blobs against the sky.

Goog found his camera lying in the mud near where he and Aldo had fought. He scooped it up and pulled a leaf from the lens. Looking through the viewfinder, he imagined himself back at the Bight.

If he concentrated carefully, he could see Castro rising over the waves. Further back, he could see him in Port Campbell, talking with the beards at the pub. It was like pulling back the focus until the whole picture was revealed. Castro at Johanna, at the going-away party, the morning when this trip had been planned; and before, long before, when as children they had grabbed foamies and braved the shorey at Torquay. Vegemite sangers at playtime. Iceblocks and zinc cream on hot summer afternoons. A friendship that had seemed to be forever. But now it was over and it was time to move forward. There was only one thing left to do. Get to Margaret River. Surf the break for Castro and lay his memory to rest.

Goog pulled his eye away from the camera and hung it around his neck. He looked up the tree. He had left part of himself behind at the foot of that Nullarbor ladder. It was time to recover that piece. To climb back up the ladder and surface from the dark world he had plunged into nearly a week before.

Goog grabbed a peg with his hand and swung his foot up onto the first rung. The peg was steel and almost unbearably cold on his palm. At the spot where it had been rammed into the tree's bark, Goog could see a lump like a raised vaccination scar. He swung his other leg free of the ground and stood there for a while, testing the rung for strength. If he kept his feet near the trunk, the rung would be strong enough to hold his weight, but out near the edge he could imagine the flex in the steel rod. Shutting himself off from the thought of danger, he clenched his teeth and climbed quickly, mechanically, for ten or more rungs. He only stopped when his head began to spin and he realised he hadn't breathed since leaving the ground.

What would it feel like to fall here? It would not be the slow graceful arc Goog had imagined that day on the cliff, above the growling waters of the Bight. There, the air was clear and buoyant with salt. There, he had the ocean to mourn him. He had space to scream, room to scrape at the sky with wide-spread fingers. Here, branches and steel rods would snag his falling body. Here, the sky was closed over like a scab. There were flocks of screeching parrots and the pocking sound of rain on wet leaves.

That day, he'd had Castro to save him. Castro the safety net. Even if Goog had fallen, his friend would have watched him go. If he fell now, who would listen to his cry? Aldo was gone and Jasper was as slippery as the air he was climbing through. Goog hated them both. He hated himself for beginning this climb but, even as he was thinking this, his limbs were carrying him higher up the tree. If he slipped, his body would shatter like a bottle. His insides would coat the base of the tree like logger's paint. His breath would be forced out of him and the wind would steal it. The ground was too far below.

The rungs burnt his fingers like ice. The breeze raked across his face, chilled the sweat that was pouring from him. His legs were drained of power.

He closed his eyes and took a snapshot of the past. Imagining the folded layers of rock and the rough wooden ladders of the Bight, he dragged his body up. Up from the memories that trapped him. Up to where the air was sweet and everything was possible once again.

Goog's fingers touched wet boards and, opening his eyes, he saw the lookout. He could hear the happy chatter of the bearded-jumpers and the pinging of bellbirds. His heart was made of air, so buoyant he felt it would carry him over the tree-tops and out to the coast where he belonged. He had made it. He had climbed to the top. He had beaten his fear. His heart had risen from where he had abandoned it at the foot of the Nullarbor cliff.

When he closed his eyes again, he could feel the slow rhythm of the sea inside him. He could see Castro rising and falling over sharp lines of swell, dolphins racing below him. The glassy perfection of waves sucking at white sand. He would carry this with him forever.

Goog dragged himself onto the platform. The view across the tops of the trees spun his head, but he was euphoric. The bearded-jumpers clapped him on the back and passed him the soggy end of the joint they had been smoking. Goog accepted it but walked to the guardrail and dropped it quietly over the edge.

From this height, the forest looked like a carpet of soft grass. His brain was happy that there seemed to be something solid within an easy drop. Of course it was a trick. If he jumped, he would fall through the branches and leaves as if they were cloud. But that was the secret of this bravery – tricking your brain into believing the impossible, believing you could do it, no matter what.

'Goog.' Aldo's meaty paw dropped onto his shoulder. 'We're going to be okay now, aren't we?'

Goog looked at Aldo and then past him to Jasper leaning confidently against the rail. Jasper's long fingers came around Aldo's arm.

'You're going to be fine, Aldo,' he said.

Greg Leary – one-hour processing. Goog flipped open the pack and pulled out the photos. The first showed Aldo and the bearded-jumpers with their arms round each others' shoulders like a football team. The next one looked like a softly rolling sea, until you looked closely and realised it was the forest canopy. They were all out of order; Goog hated it when the processing dorks looked at his films. Next was Goog and Aldo back at the Kingswood – Jasper had taken it and it was blurry and underexposed, with Goog's feet cut at the ankles. There were no photos of Jasper.

Goog riffled through the pack. Near the end, he found one of Castro at camp, the night before his disappearance. It was the only one – frame one. Castro smiling his stupid smile, the light of the fire on his face. He was drinking from a tin mug.

While they were up the Gloucester Tree, someone had broken into the car and taken Goog's camera bag. Luckily he had his camera with him, but all the film he had shot since leaving Torquay was gone. All his photos from the trip, except for the film he had loaded that night on the cliffs above *Ladders*. He had panicked when he discovered the rolls were missing. But then he realised he had all the images stored inside him. That it was enough just to remember. No one could steal memories, not even Jasper.

Jasper was over at the payphone, *dealing with some business*, as he put it. Aldo came back to the table, three beers clustered in his big hands. He clonked them down on the table, spilling the tops off them, and peered over Goog's shoulder at the photo of Castro. His fat thumb came over the back of the print and pulled it out of Goog's grasp.

'Can I have this?' he asked, dropping it in a pool of beer froth on the table.

Goog didn't know if he was ready to let go of this last real image. 'I'll get you a copy made.'

'No, I want this one, Goog.' Aldo stabbed his finger at the photo and it went under the puddle of beer.

Goog was too weary for a fight. 'Take it. It's yours.'

Jasper returned from the payphone. 'So, tomorrow, it's Margaret River. Your journey's nearly over. You chaps have had a fair trip. Bet you'll be glad to get a surf in.'

Goog nodded and sipped at his beer. He wished Jasper would just disappear. He was sick of their stalemate.

Someone put 'Khe Sahn' on the jukebox and Aldo began to sing, 'Sappas . . . round . . . san . . . sold . . . soul . . . market man . . .' Just the words he could remember.

When Goog got up and went to the toilet, the blokes at the pool table were playing air guitar with their cues and singing along to the song.

At the trough, the token drunk stood with one hand against the wall, pissing on his shoes. He eyed Goog up as he approached the urinal. There was a smell of stale urine and trough-lollies.

'Yer not from here, are *ya*!' He shouted the last word so loudly that Goog, who had just started to pee, nearly did it on the man's leg. The man finished and zipped up his fly. His shirt hung out the front like a wrongly pinned tail.

'No, mate, I'm from Torquay.' There was a tiredness in

Goog's voice that he couldn't cover. He didn't want to be talking to this bloke.

'Where's at en? Where zit?'

The drunk apparently wasn't embarrassed to be talking to Goog and his performing penis. But Goog, feeling a little shy, turned into the corner of the trough.

'Victoria, mate. Near Melbourne.'

'Melbourne. Don't bloody talk to me about Melbourne. I know Melbourne. Bloody shishole.'

'I said *near* Melbourne.' Goog wished he'd piss off. Why were these drunks always attracted to him? Was he some kind of dero magnet?

'Yeah, I knew a bloke from around that way. Geelong or somebloodyplace. Maybe that place you're from. Yeah, he was over there and then he came over to Kal, to work in the mines. Always crapping on bout the beach and stuff. Used to call him Bleary, name was something Leary, y'see. Leary rhymes with Bleary, dunnit?' He cocked his head on one side. 'Boy, could that man put away the piss. Bit of a no-hoper. Bit of a dero.'

Goog looked at the man and felt sickness rising inside him. Did this drunk know his old man? He pushed past him and into the pub, making straight for where Aldo and Jasper were sitting. 'Let's get on the road,' he said and threw back his beer as he stood there.

'You gotta be jokin, Goog. We just got here. Sit down, I'll get you another beer.' Aldo had the photo of Castro in the top pocket of his shirt. A clean shirt, Goog noticed. Had Jasper insisted? He watched Aldo go to the bar.

Jasper said, 'Goog, I think you'd better just sit down. From what Aldo says, you've been doing all the driving and you haven't slept much. We'll stay here the night and we'll get to

Margaret River in the morning.' He looked Goog in the eye. 'You're not on the run from those fears again are you? I thought you'd sorted all that.' He sipped at his beer and placed it carefully on the beer mat. 'We'll rest up and get going tomorrow.'

Goog made a grab at the car keys sitting on the table in front of Jasper. 'No. We're going now! You're not calling the shots any more.'

Jasper's hand came down on top of the keys. 'I can't let you do that, Goog. I need that computer disk. You need the information. Let's do that deal. I'm sure if I have longer with Aldo I'll get what I need for free.'

Goog turned around to look for help or a weapon or something. The drunk was lunging out of the toilets just as Aldo came back with another round of drinks. The thought that this pathetic dero may have known his dad was one too many fears for Goog to face on this trip. Goog grabbed Aldo's arm, spilling beer over the table. 'Aldo, please, we've got to go. It's important that we get to Margaret River.' Goog was desperate. He needed an ally and Aldo was the closest thing he had. 'Come on, Aldo.'

Aldo just looked at him with his big stupid face.

Goog used his last card. 'Castro would have wanted us to finish this.'

'And you will finish it. Tomorrow.' Jasper was looking directly at Aldo. He picked up his beer and took a sip. Frost ran down the glass and a drip fell on the table.

But Goog's trump card had won the hand and Aldo said, 'We should go.'

Jasper shook his head. 'Okay, you win this one,' he said. 'But I'm not driving.'

'I'm going to drive,' said Goog. Jasper handed the keys over to him, lingering just a little on the exchange.

Jasper said, 'We've still got some distance to go and I *am* going to get what I want.'

But at least as he said it they were moving. Clearing out of the pub, away from the toilet-drunk and his seedy memories.

14

MARGARET RIVER

First Castro had wanted this beach. Then Goog had needed it. This beach had drawn Aldo's old Kingswood over four thousand kilometres. This beach started and finished it all.

They arrived at night because of Goog's impatience. Jasper said nothing and Aldo quickly fell asleep. Goog walked down to the beach and sat in the sand, then opened his mouth to the rain and let it hit the back of his throat. At the start of the trip he had imagined arriving on a sunny morning. The wind was offshore (it always was in dreams) and the locals smiled as they paddled out to six-foot peaks. Even later, when Castro was gone, he had managed to work that dream to keep him going. On the days when they hadn't seen water – at Kalgoorlie, in the flat calm of the desert – Goog had closed his eyes and imagined being here.

The clouds began to shift over the sky and expose the half moon. The sound of the waves was light, hush-hush-hushing at the shore. It was the sound of small surf, or no surf, the sound of defeat. Goog's toes gripped the sand. The sky was clearing and the edges of the clouds were fringed in yellow light. Slowly the moon bent down towards the horizon and lit a path across the sea to the beach.

Goog undid the ockie straps around his boardbag, lifted it quietly down from the roof and sat it on the tar.

'What are you doing?' Jasper had come from the direction of the toilet block.

Goog slipped his board out of its cover and ran his hands down the rails. 'I'm going surfing.'

Jasper stood between him and the car. 'It's still dark, Goog.'

'I came here to go surfing.'

Aldo woke up and came outside. 'What's up, Goog?'

'Nothing, Aldo. Go back to sleep.'

'He's going surfing,' said Jasper.

Aldo sputtered, 'Y-you can't, Goog. It's night. There'll be sharks and shit. You can't.'

Jasper said, 'Leave him, Aldo. He knows what he's doing,' and pushed Aldo back into the car.

Goog opened the tailgate window and grabbed his bag. Jasper got in the car beside Aldo and turned on the light. Goog could hear them muttering as he pulled out his wettie. The smell of neoprene and the feelings it dredged up were a shock to him. Surfing had always smelled like the sea, like salt and sea-weed, a healthy smell. But this chemical smell of rubber, like day-old piss, dragged him back to carparks and beaches, to reefs and points. It slapped him with Castro's smile, his hand-stands on the high-tide mark, the seal-bark of his laugh. And the oil-smooth water filled with shards of fibreglass.

Goog blinked away the memory and undressed quickly. He dragged his wetsuit on, and picked up his clothes and went to put them in the back of the car. As he did so, he kicked a pile of junk that had dropped out of his bag – his dad's postcard of Kalgoorlie two-up, a lump of surfwax and the map to *Elephants*. He bundled these memories in his clothes and chucked them in the back of the car. Reaching in, he noticed Jasper flipping a big copper coin through his fingers and reading Aldo something from a thick book.

> *'Six at the top means:*
> *One must go through the water.*
> *It goes over one's head.*
> *Misfortune. No Blame.'*

Jasper turned sideways to Aldo and nodded like a living Buddha. *Bullshit*, Goog thought, *fucking bullshit*. Jasper was a cheap fake and Goog wondered how he had held so much power over the three of them, why they had been so afraid of him. He rolled up the tailgate window and grabbed his board from the ground.

The sand was wet. If it were dry, this sand would cough and squeak under his feet, but he had to settle for silence. Around the edges of the sky, out to sea and at the tips of the beach, the clouds were gathering again. The sea was like treacle, rolling slowly against the beach. Hush . . . hush . . . hush . . . hush. There was half a metre of swell, maybe less. It wasn't even breaking out past the shorebreak. But it was important to finish this thing properly. Goog knew that.

He had expected the sea to be warm. This was the Indian Ocean, the ocean of turquoise barrels. But it was, in reality, cold and sucking blackly at the beach. He walked out until he was up to his waist in water and his balls had pulled up inside him, then, dragging his board beneath him, he lay on his belly and began to paddle out to where the fat humps of waves were lazily rising and falling without breaking.

Halfway out, a breakaway cloud tackled the moon. For a while Goog could see nothing. But gradually his eyes grew used to the blackness and the sea appeared to become clearer until he could see below the surface, down to where dark shapes were moving. This was what had lured Castro the night of his peyote experience.

Goog had to know what had happened to him that night and what had happened to him the next day, out in the Southern Ocean. There was no way Jasper was going to supply those answers. Not for free.

Undoing his legrope, Goog rolled off his board and slipped under. He swam down until his fingers scraped on rock. He followed the reef along until a hole appeared, just a dark stain on a black cloth. Inside, something moved. Something big and muscular. The air was beginning to go stale in Goog's lungs. His chest was beginning to hurt. But he couldn't swim for the surface.

He didn't feel scared. He felt calm and strangely happy. There was a glow at the back of the hole now, that made him want to go inside, made him want to touch it. Goog remembered a story his dad had told him about phosphorescence and how tonnes of the stuff had washed up once on Sydney beaches. How dogs had left luminous footprints on the sand. Goog had laughed at the story and told his dad he was mad.

Goog now knew why Castro had swum down. He had gone to be with his deepest fears. Because that was what Castro did, that was what he had learnt to do in his eighteen years. When he faced those fears, they were no longer real.

Suddenly, the whole seafloor was alive with light. Goog could see brittle-stars and jellyfish and the bulky shapes of grouper wandering through the kelp forests. The moon was shining from above, from the real world. Goog realised he was nearly out of air, he had to get back to the surface.

His first snatch of oxygen was cold and sweet. His board was floating nearby and he swam over and pulled himself onto it.

He felt the square of plastic, uncomfortable in the shoulder of his wetsuit, cutting through his rash-vest and into his shoulder blade. He unzipped his wettie and pulled out the Zip disk. This was what Jasper had wanted. He had some heavy knowledge to trade for this small square of plastic, a story about Castro, real or invented. Goog weighed the Zip in his hand. He thought about all it contained, the bytes of hate burnt into its magnetic surface. Castro was gone and there was no bringing him back. He knew what Castro would have wanted him to do.

Goog hurled the disk as far as he could. It skimmed over the water, sending up arrows of light. Then it sank. Down, like the flakes of Castro's board. Swallowed by the ocean.

The Kingswood was gone and with it Jasper and Aldo. The only things left in the carpark were Goog's camera and the phone card his mum had given him the day he left Torquay.

He picked up the camera – was this his future? If he chose that path, then it was time to leave the past behind, time to look at the world in a new way. He needed to stop using the camera as a shield and open himself up to the world.

And then the phone card – *classic margaret river w.a.* – his link to the past. Torquay. Home. He had come a long way in two weeks. Further than he ever thought he would. Much further than the four-thousand-plus kilometres they had travelled.

He laid the camera and the phone card side by side on the ground and looked over to where the Kingswood had been. Patches of oil were rainbowing on the wet bitumen – sump, gearbox and diff.

He was free now, free to choose, but he needed to act quickly. Jasper wasn't stupid. But he would find out Aldo was. He would discover that Aldo knew very little about the Zip disk; the last time he had seen it was in Norseman. Jasper would realise Goog had been hiding it and then they would be back. The shit would really hit the fan when Goog told him about tossing the disk to the ocean.

A Maui campervan arrived. It stopped and a light went on inside. Someone peered out of the window. A moment later, a woman appeared, wrapped from head to toe in Gore-Tex and carrying a coffee mug. When she got near, Goog realised it was one of the Germans from the Twelve Apostles. The mother. She put the mug down beside Goog and smiled.

'Kaffee?' she said.

Goog picked up the mug and said, 'Thank you.'

'Velkom.' She nodded and walked back to the campervan.

Goog sculled the warm, sweet coffee, carried the mug back to the van and knocked on the door.

'Ja?' Papa appeared at the door, with his daughter smiling over his shoulder.

'Thanks for the coffee,' said Goog, handing back the mug.

'Velkom.' Papa looked at Goog, at the sand covering his face. He looked past Goog to his board, camera and phone card lying in the empty carpark. 'Come in,' he said.

The camper was warm inside. Midnight Oil blared from the

stereo. Papa turned it down and handed Goog a towel, a pair of tracksuit pants and a fleecy top, then pushed him towards the shower.

When Goog returned he was pink from the hot water. The Germans were huddled around the coffee table, talking in whispers. He smiled at them.

Papa grinned back, 'Ah, Mr Surfie is dry, ja? Alles güt! We see a lot of fery veird sights but this surfie things is fery fery veird.' Papa rumpled his brow at Goog, to show just how weird he thought it was. 'Ja, veird. In Nullarbor Desert, one surfie he is hitchinghiking vit vetsuit. Vetsuit in desert. Hitchinghiking! Haha.' Papa glanced at his brother and they both broke into huge shoulder-spasm laughs.

Seeing Goog's confusion, Mama and her daughter smiled apologetically.

The daughter said, 'It is true. Like Papa said, we were driving across the Nullarbor and we saw this surfer. He looked like a surfer but he had no board. He was on the other side of the road and he was wearing a wetsuit. Weird, huh?' She flashed her braces at Goog and popped her bubblegum.

'Yeah, that's weird,' said Goog. 'Real weird.'

Papa slapped him on the back. 'So ve take you to hotel, ja?'

Goog could hardly speak. The shock of what they had told him rocked his world again. 'Youth hostel will do . . . thanks . . . yeah.'

There was a knock at the door. When Mama opened it, a man with skanky dreadlocks was holding Goog's board, camera and phone card.

'These yours, guys?' he asked and poked the nose of the board into the doorway.

Goog jumped up. 'Yeah, they're mine. Thanks, man.'

'Thascool. Should be a little more careful with your gear, dude. Nearly ran over it.'

'Yeah, I will. Thanks.' Goog grabbed his stuff and shut the door.

On the road to the hostel, Goog watched the slanting spears of rain. Farmland, winery signs, wire fences – all dulled by the tinted glass of the Maui. He closed his eyes against all of it and in a bright flash he saw Aldo and Jasper. They were out on the open road, the windows in the Kingswood wound fully down, air rocketing in on them. 'Khe Sanh' was on the radio and they were both singing at the top of their lungs. They were moving away from him at a hundred clicks. Goog smiled at the image, wished it into reality. That was the secret of bravery – tricking your brain into believing the impossible.

The hostel manager dragged herself away from her cowboy book and signed Goog in. When she had fitted him in neat columns, she stuck the pen behind her ear and said, 'Do you want a job? Cleaning rooms, painting, running the bus into town, that kind of thing. Can't pay much but you can have a bed for free.'

Goog leant against his board, looking down at the plastic bag the Germans had given him for his wetsuit, camera and phone card.

'Can I think about it?'

'Sure, but I need to know before tonight. We're expecting a bus load of Swedes. One of them will do as good as you.' She picked up her cowboy book and opened it to cover her face.

On the way to the mixed dorm, Goog stopped at the phone. He rummaged in his bag and got out his phone card. There were only two numbers to call – Marcella or Mum. Marcella told him to call if he got his shit together. Well, he had.

The phone was ringing out. He shut his eyes and imagined the signal travelling across the desert. Past Kalgoorlie choked with utes and blue singlets. Through Norseman, the counter lady still pouring bottomless tea. Past the turnoff to *Ladders* without even pausing. Through Adelaide and past its gang of dangerous skinheads and out down the Great Ocean Road.

'Mum . . . yeah, Mum, it's me . . . Yeah, look I'm fine . . . I know, Castro's gone, Mum . . . I will, I'll go to the police in the morning . . . Margaret River . . . Yeah, I'm okay . . . how's Priya? . . . Mum, I don't want to talk to Marcella . . . because it's over between us . . . just tell her I'm not coming home . . . Yes, it's true . . . I'm going to stay here for a while, save up some cash and then who knows, maybe Indo. Take some photos, write some things . . . I know it won't be the same without Castro, Mum, I know . . . of course I miss him . . . Mum, I gotta go. Kiss Priya for me. I'll call you later . . . Yeah, of course I'll take care . . . I love you too, bye.'

Dropping the receiver back into the cradle, he felt the connection sever. Now he had made the choice, he felt better, stronger, than ever before. He got his camera out of his bag and hung it around his neck. Picking up his board, the not-quite-rhino-chaser, he went to find his bed.

On the wall outside the toilets he saw a cork noticeboard. He couldn't help looking at the traveller's posts.

Lift Offered: 1 female to Darwin. Vegie non-smoker.
Must have own tent.

Perth 2 seats leaving 22/7 share petrol and expenses.
Bus ticket 3 mths left cheap $200 ono.

And then Goog spotted something. An envelope that made his heart high-jump into his throat and then dump into his stomach. It was addressed:

G & A
Backpackers
Margaret River
W.A.
Australia

Someone had written in red pen: *Try Custard Sam's Backpackers.*

The postage stamp was printed on cheap paper in lurid colours – a shadow puppet, its profile broken by the postmark. *G & A* – it could be just a coincidence.

Goog pulled the envelope off the board and flipped it over. No return address. He looked back into the TV room where some Poms were channel surfing for more soap, looked out to the check-in counter, where the manager was in the middle of an encounter with a low-down gunslinger by the name of Jed. No one was watching as Goog put his finger under the flap of the envelope and prised it up.

The first thing he pulled out was a postcard of Uluwatu Peak at full scream. Indonesian madness, a steep, deep barrelling wave spitting over sharp coral. There was a guy slotted in the green room, speed-crouching, waiting for the almost certain shutdown. Castro had told Goog that one in three barrels shut down at *The Peak*, and this one looked like it would.

Goog flipped the card over but there was no message. He turned it back to the picture. The guy behind the barelling wave was stroking for the next one, a perfect sharp beast that was just starting to pitch. It was a ten-foot day, easy, and there were lines set up forever.

This was the wave that Castro had wanted, above all others. On those Torquay onshore days, he would tell Goog and Aldo how the entry to the break was down through the cave, a near-vertical drop into the ocean. And they would tell him to shut up, because everyone knew that. Then Castro would add something extra, one slip at a time. Once he had told them how, on a full-moon tide, the cave was extra dangerous. And when big days coincided with a full moon, then the only place to get out of the water was back through the cave. The beach completely disappeared. Only the cliffs remained, with waves smacking up against them. Timing and luck were needed because it was real easy to get swept past the cave or onto the rocks. Castro had studied that break. He had made that break his religion.

There was something else in the envelope, a small chunky triangle of folded paper. Goog poked his fingers in like tweezers and extracted the bundle. The writing on the paper was tiny. As he unfolded the triangles, the paper expanded, revealing more and more words.

I argued I had no quar —

—- my bent character was to talk —

And one word at the top point of the second triangle:

— peyote.

Goog opened the paper quickly, his fingers numb on the folds, too big to deal with the thinness of the paper. At the fourth unfolding the paper turned into a square – the basis of most origami – the number *51* on a cuff, turned over along one edge. As Goog unfolded the cuff and flipped the paper over, he saw the words *The Teachings* written opposite the number. Another half fold and he held the yellowed page of a book between his fingers. Just under halfway down, below the centre fold, there was a quote underlined in red pen:

All this is very easy to understand. Fear is the first natural enemy a man must overcome on his path to knowledge. Besides, you are curious. That evens up the score. And you must learn in spite of yourself; that's the rule.

It was Castro's Castaneda book, *The Teachings of Don Juan*. The one he had been reading as they crossed the Paddock. Goog crumpled the page in his hand until he felt he was absorbing the words. Absorbing them into his palm, as Castro had done with the cuttlefish symbols the night before his death – a death surrounded with so much mystery, so much uncertainty, that Goog didn't know what to believe any more.

He would never know what had happened between Jasper and Castro that night in the desert. What they had talked about and planned under the peyote moon, while Goog and Aldo lay drugged-out on the sand.

And somehow it didn't matter. Either way, Castro was gone and Goog was on his own. He hoped Castro was alive but he couldn't spend the rest of his life waiting to find out.

Goog unfolded his hand and looked at the crumpled page, then down to the floor where the envelope lay. He picked it up and held it to the light. The stamp was Indonesian for sure. The address was looped in Castro's long fluid script.

It had only been a week since he had disappeared. There was too much land, too much sea to cover in that amount of time.

But you could come a long way in a week.

ABOUT THE AUTHOR

Neil Grant was born in Scotland and spent his teenage years learning to speak Australian. A large part of his adult life has been spent travelling and working on his résumé. On occasion, he has been an instrument steriliser, a forklift driver, a banana picker, a dishwasher and a brickie's labourer. He wishes he lived on the coast with his wife Ingrid and daughter Emma, but for now Diamond Creek in Victoria will do. Neil's board is so ancient that other surfers recognise it as an antique.

His love of the water and wild places has led him to write about those things.